STELLA, UNTIL YOU

IRON ORCHIDS

DANIELLE NORMAN

STELLA, UNTIL YOU

Everyone sees me as sassy, outspoken, and unafraid of
anything.
But the truth is, I'm scared.
Scared of being rejected by Doctor Tristan Christakos.

When we are both sent to a conference, our worlds collide.

It was one week in Vegas.
Two people, me and Dr. Christakos.
And three possible outcomes.
Spend it together.
Spend it separated.
Or, uncover a secret so big it shakes our worlds.

I wished that we would have known about option three
before we choose the other.
When the secret comes out, who will be left standing, and
will Tristan still be there for me?

Look, look, look Linda, listen to me, I do not write porn. I write steamy romance. You have no clue what you're talking about. Take a moment and read, maybe you'll learn what your husband would like.

∾

To the group of drunken women, that I'm fortunate to call friends... Otherwise known as: Charlie Hunnam's motherfucking dragon, the legal eagle, the Swedish chef, the Indian Princess, Thorne in my side, and Windsor Palace: I fucking love you. Now do NOT make me cry again.

"Love is a misunderstanding between two fools."
— Oscar Wilde

UNTIL

To my wonderful readers, thank you for riding along on this wild Iron Orchids ride, my very first romance series. A few things before you begin.

I beg you from the bottom of my heart to please not leave any spoilers in reviews or on social media. I had such a fun time figuring out how to fuck with you, that I want everyone to have the same experience when they read it for the first time. Remember that when you are in Chapter Five and the world is exactly how you want it…bwahaha. Yeah, I'm a bitch, but hey, I created Stella after all.

CHEERS,
Dani

STELLA

I scanned the charts and briefly looked up at the patients.

"Sick. Sick. Faking. Asshole. Drama queen. Sick."

Sometimes, I felt like the fucking Grinch doling out jury duty summonses. I grabbed the information for my first patient and headed to room seven . . . okay, let's be honest, I headed into the curtained off section we called room seven.

Gotta love the ER.

It stank of disinfectant and most of the people who walked in the door were idiots, but I loved it here . . . at the hospital, as in I loved my job as a nurse, not in the ER. I'd much rather be up in neonatal, but I couldn't. I just couldn't stand seeing—

"Stella?"

Mrs. Cameron, an administrator with the hospital, was standing behind me. The woman had to be in her early fifties, but the way she dressed and styled her hair—a blue polyester pantsuit and an overly processed blonde bob that resembled a football helmet—made her look as if she were in her early seventies. She had a look on her face, one that I'd seen a hundred times, it said, *I have no clue what to make of you.*

"Yes?"

"When you're done with this patient, can you please meet me in my office?"

"Sure. Give me five minutes." I retuned my attention to the patient, and he was giving me a stare, you know one of those, *should I trust you with my life because you're getting ready to get in trouble.* He was totally questioning my competence. Well, listen here, motherfucker, I was as competent as they came. "What?" I snapped at him.

Okay, that wasn't exactly professional, but give me a break.

"Sounds like you're in trouble. Maybe I should have a different nurse." He rolled his eyes as he said that, totally dismissing me.

"Sure, why not. I'm a RN, any mommy could have helped you, and it wouldn't have cost you a grand. You have a splinter, that's all. Most normal people don't come to the hospital for those kinds of things."

Okay, maybe adding normal was wrong, but hey, it was better than what I really wanted to say, which was something along the lines of him being an overgrown man-child, and I felt sorry for the woman who got saddled with his sorry ass.

Recording his vitals information into his chart, I filed it for the doctor then headed to the charge nurse. "Hey, can you have someone cover my patients? I need to run to the admin offices."

"You're all set, Stella, Mrs. Cameron already said that she needed you. Just hurry back."

"Thanks."

Lost in my own world, pondering why I was being called to the admin offices, I almost ran into one of the ER doctors.

"You look radiant this morning," he said as he walked by,

flashing me a smile. He was trying desperately to be the hospital's version of Doctor McDreamy. He might have accomplished it if it weren't for one man, a gorgeous Greek neonatologist who I had deemed Dr. McCreamy. He was the reason I was no longer over at the Women and Children's Center, and it wasn't because he hated me or because I couldn't stand him—quite the opposite, actually. When he was around, I tended to want to lose my clothes. One time, I actually lost my head and acted on it, and . . . well, yeah. I couldn't work there anymore.

As I turned down the last corridor, my heartbeat picked up speed as it hit me because there was a chance this call to admin wouldn't be good. Had they heard about what happened?

No. If they had, they would have had someone from human resources come scoop me up.

Maybe I was being escorted out for doing something wrong. Sure, I was sarcastic, but I hadn't told anyone to fuck off, at least, I didn't think I had. I mean, come on, I was a nurse, and even in the twenty-first century the profession was dominated by women, which meant one thing—cattiness. So, I guessed that I could have pissed off a coworker, those bitches be trippin', and no, I didn't push any of them.

Stopping in front of the large faux-wood door that read: Staff Administration, I took a deep breath and then knocked.

"Come in."

One step into the room, I froze because sitting in one of the chairs was Dr. McCreamy, otherwise known as Tristan Christakos, the most gorgeous man to ever walk the planet, the bane of my existence, and the best one-night stand ever. Yeah, he was a mistake that I'd happily make or should I say *do* again.

Fuck.

Tristan stood when I entered, as his damn well-bred,

gentlemanly self had to do, which only made me want to jump him even more. To make matters worse, he was wearing a devilishly wicked smirk on his lips that made all of my parts take notice.

"Stella, have a seat." Louise Cameron's back was ramrod straight as she sat in her high-back, black pleather chair. If I were to base my visit on her posture alone, I would say I was about to be canned.

The hospital had a no fraternization policy. Although, they had allowed married couples to work for the same hospital in the past, this all had to be reported to admin, and they ultimately decided whether or not to keep both employees. In situations like this when it was between a doctor and a nurse, they usually ended up keeping the doctor since nurses were a dime a dozen. Was that fair? Hell no.

I could already feel the ire in me building and was ready to fight or at least not go down without a fight.

I moved to the chair opposite Tristan and plopped down. Okay, I knew that I possessed little to no grace when I did that, but whatever, I was pissed. Turning to face him, the heat in me rose as he continued to smirk. The asshole *smirked*. He knew we were busted and he was safe. I'd never imagined him being so cruel.

But fuck a duck if the man still wasn't gorgeous. His eyes were the color of fresh coffee, untainted by cream. And his skin . . . well, that was a different story, it was cream with a dash of coffee.

"Stella," Mrs. Cameron began, "as you are aware, the hospital is building a genetics study center in the hopes of being able to more easily find donor matches. Every year, it seems that there is a bigger strain on our match and donor resources. Not only from the state of perpetual emergency that we seem to be in but also our advance technology in ultrasound imaging. As you know, we are able to detect some birth defects as early as the first heart beat. We feel that it is important as a level one trauma unit and a level-three neonatal ward that we have this resource available to us twenty-four seven. We've been sending doctors to different training sessions so they are up to date with all the current technologies and tests."

Tristan cleared his throat, and I turned my attention back to him. "You may not be aware of this, Stella, but my interest has always been with trying to negate the rise in genetic birth defects that we see in our high-risk unit. But after the strain on our resource bank for tissue, marrow, and blood, my research was halted. This new genetic center will help me continue my focus."

I listened to Tristan's explanation, but none of this made sense. Sure, his reasoning made sense, but where I was lost was what in the hell any of this had to do with me. My face must have shown my confusion because Mrs. Cameron finally slid a file folder to me.

"There is a pediatric genetics conference in Las Vegas next week, and we've been on the waiting list. Yesterday, we found out that there had been a cancellation and that Dr. Christakos has been invited. He has been asked to bring a nurse or assistant, and he tells me that the two of you worked well together when you were over in the Women and Children's Center."

I nodded because we had worked well together, and she smiled.

"He'd like you to accompany him to the conference and act as his assistant moving forward as we get the genetic center established."

Slow down there, Polyester, he what?

He wanted me to work with him?

He wanted me to go to Vegas?

Me. Tristan. In Vegas? Fuck yeah, where did I sign?

Shaking my head, I turned to look at the olive skin Adonis with chocolate eyes that made me want to get on my knees and say ten Hail Marys and praise sweet baby Jesus.

Shit. I was staring. Smacking my lips, I cleared my throat and then tried again. "Sure, tell me whatever you need," I said and watched as the corners of Tristan's lips pulled into an almost challenging smile. I had no clue what he was challenging me to, but he knew better than to yank my chain because, let's face it, I yanked harder, and of the two of us, he was the only one with something to grab ahold of and tug.

He must have read my mind or followed my line of sight because he shifted away from me just a bit.

Yeah, that's right, pretty boy, I thought and then smirked back.

"Perfect. Inside that folder is your itinerary. We follow the government posted per diem rate, so please check the website. I believe the last I looked it was roughly two hundred dollars a day that included lodging and meals. So, anything over that is on you. Are you both okay with that?"

I nodded and then looked at Tristan. "Absolutely," he agreed.

"I'll have someone book your flights and forward you the tickets. Where should we email them to?"

"You can email them both to me," Tristan spoke before I had gathered my sense to say something.

Mrs. Cameron jotted down a few notes and then looked back up. "Thank you, Dr. Christakos, why don't you and Miss Lang take this to your office and work out any final details?"

Tristan stood, thanked Louise Cameron for her time, and gestured for me to go ahead of him. I stood, albeit on shaky legs, and followed him out of the office. He didn't say a word to me. We just walked side by side, our steps in sync.

Fuck that, I double-stepped, and it knocked us out of

sync. He sped up and put us back into synchronization. I was five-foot-ten, so even though Tristan was tall, he was only four inches taller than I was. I lunged forward, taking a larger than normal step, and moved Tristan firmly behind me.

Damn. He took a giant step and came forward until we were, once again, in unison and standing side by fucking side. We passed by a couple of nurses, who stopped to stare at the spectacle we were making, and I shot them a wink. There was no way I was going to allow him to get ahead of me. I'd already gone along with his idea to just pretend we hadn't had hot sex on his desk, but that didn't mean it didn't burn my crawl, I wasn't going to allow him to dictate that we walked side by side.

Sometimes, there is just too much damn joy in the little wins.

As we walked in silence, still battling back and forth over our pace, I thought—okay, okay . . . I plotted over how to get the upper hand.

Juvenile as it may be, I was going to take the best option, which was to stop and pretend to tie my shoe.

Tristan stopped and waited just like the proper gentleman I knew he was. After a second, I grabbed the tail on one lace of his shoe and yanked. While he stood there, probably trying to decide if I'd really just done what I'd done, I laughed and bolted for the bank of elevators.

Ignoring the other people on the elevator, I pressed the button for the third floor where his office was located and waited for the doors to close. Maybe I was doing this for more than payback over his wanting to forget that we'd had one night of the hottest sex ever or maybe it was something profound. Yeah . . . I was going with profound like it was my way to stand up to misogynistic assholes. Only problem was, Tristan supported women's rights as much as I did. So, back to my question . . . why? Oh, I remember . . . because he was a man and, as such, I must always remind him that he was never quite as good as a woman. I mentally patted myself on the back and then stepped out of the elevator, only to slam right into someone walking by.

"Watch where you're going." The deep timbre from the man's voice rippled through me, and I didn't have to look up to see who I'd tripped over because I already knew. The kicker? He beat me up to the third floor without even bothering to tie his damn shoe.

"Hi, Tristan, I mean, Dr. Christakos."

His breath tickled the side of my neck and caused me to flinch. "I like when you call me Tristan better. In fact, I like when you shout Tristan most of all." He almost purred.

Ripping myself from his hold, I stood straight, my cheeks burning because, yes, he knew what that sounded like. Three months ago in his office, on his desk, after a late night. Our emotions were high, and we'd both been on shift almost twenty hours because of a multiple-car accident near Disney. I'd assisted Tristan with a baby, the mom had been six months pregnant when she suffered a placental abruption in the accident. Her injuries were critical, and while surgeons had done everything possible to save her, she didn't make it. Tristan and I had helped to deliver the baby via emergency C-section.

The image of the husband leaning over the infant was burned into the backs of my eyelids, and I could still hear him crying softly and saying that at least his wife would live on through their son.

The little boy was beautiful, tiny but a fighter. I thought he was going to make it, and I know that Tristan did, too. We both stayed there for hours, watching and waiting because neither of us wanted to leave, each of us were so vested in this young fighter.

But . . . ten hours after we brought him into this world, I was standing next to Tristan as he told the father that the little boy was with his mother.

We'd gone back to Tristan's office, emotionally and physically exhausted but still flooded with adrenaline. It was that, mixed with years of pent-up sexual frustration and the intense need to feel something other than the heartbreaking loss that had led to one unforgettable night on his desk, hell, we hadn't even locked the door in the hurry to feed our passion.

As much as I wanted to blame it all on him for being so damn sexy, I knew that I couldn't.

"Be careful, anyone walking by who sees that look on your face might think you were having a sex fantasy about me."

And, just like that, the moment was broken and the memories from three months ago were packed back away.

TRISTAN

*W*hen I pulled open the door to my parents' house, I was hit with the smell of saffron mixed with a hint of chlorine from the pool. The gust of hot air that assisted me in closing the door a tad harder than I had intended told me the back door was open and everyone was already here.

It was a Christakos family dinner and being Greek meant that there were a lot of us. So, people running in and out of the house to the pool was as common as my nieces' voices rising above the rest of the noise. I called it noise because to call it words would be a lie. None of what they were shouting about was actually discernible.

"Moro mou, you're here." My mother's Greek lilt still somehow could be heard over everyone else's. That must have been a skill acquired the moment a woman became a mother. Like it was imprinted somewhere on their DNA, and as soon as a baby landed in their arms, they gained the super-powers of knowing the difference between alligator tears and real tears, using a tone of voice that could be heard

above all else, and seeing what her child was doing without actually having to look. I headed into the kitchen and placed a kiss on my mother's cheek before waving at my sisters-in-law, Ariel and Katy, who were on the other side of the kitchen with my cousin, and then finally taking the beer that Leo held out to me.

I dropped a kiss on top of her head. "How you feeling?"

"Fine, but your brother is a Neanderthal. Did you know he made me move to an office? I'm no longer working in my own garage, nope, just office work." Leo tugged on the hem of her maternity shirt, which showed her barely there baby bump.

"It's your first, a lot of women don't show as early with their first, isn't that right, Tristan?" My brother, Ian, asked from behind me.

"That's true."

"Just because I look pregnant, it doesn't mean I've suddenly become some delicate little flower. As long as I'm not lifting heavy things, then I'm fine, right?"

She had turned her body toward me but kept her glare on Ian.

I should have known better.

"Well, that's true, too."

"But you can't be—"

I held up my hand to stop my brother mid-sentence. "Leave me out of this. There's a reason I'm not an obstetrician." I took a swig from my bottle and then headed for the lanai.

"Uncle Tristan." Not one, two, or three little girls slammed into my legs, no . . . it was four. And all four of them were soaking wet.

"Good grief, didn't any of you use a towel after getting out of the pool?" I tried to push them away, but they just giggled and clung to me tighter.

"No. Daddy said to jump on you and that you liked getting wet."

I raised one brow at my niece before turning my ire on her dad, who was trying to hold in a laugh.

"I think your dad was fibbing. Let's see if you ladies can jump in the pool and make a splash so big that you get your daddy wet."

That had them all going wide-eyed a second as the idea ran through their precocious minds before they spun and raced for the deep end of the pool.

"Well played, sir. Well played," Carter said, as we followed the four little terrors movements. One at a time they jumped, wrapping their legs and forming a tight ball trying to see who could make the largest cannonball splash.

I gave a nod to each of my brothers as I sat, and Damon grinned.

"You didn't last long in there."

"Are you fucking kidding me?" I whispered. "There were two pregnant women, one postpartum woman, Mana, and Sophie. I have way stronger self-preservation skills than that.

"Fair enough." Damon grabbed a chip out of a basket and dipped it.

"Will you stop?" I said to Kayson, who was eye-fucking his wife through the open window. "You do realize that the two of you are married, that kind of makes her like a sure thing?"

"Oooo, you have so much to learn." My brothers all laughed at my comment.

"What?"

My brothers all shook their heads at me as if they were the only ones privy to some secret club. Truth was, I wanted in that secret club. My entire family had broken off into couples except for me. The nights out that were just my brothers and me had been replaced with family events that left me the odd man out. I didn't want it that way. I wanted to be with someone . . . one person, in fact, I knew who I wanted that one person to be. Only problem was, with her it was as if our life was a metronome, always ticking, but always at the same pace, it never increased speed. Nope. At this rate, I was bound to be more reliable than the Master Clock.

"I heard something about you going to Vegas, what's up with that?" Damon asked.

"Why don't I just tell you all over dinner and save me from having to explain fifty million times, you know that Mana will want all the details as well?"

"Explain what fifty million times?" Kayson asked, finally clueing into the conversation.

I shook my head, Damon rolled his eyes and answered for me. "About his upcoming trip to Vegas."

"Ohhh." Kayson reached forward and grabbed a chip.

"Hey, are you all going to sit around on your duffs, or are you going to get your asses to work?" Pops yelled from across the lanai, and like that, the conversation was sidelined for later.

The sliding door opened and Stella came out, I wasn't shocked to see her. Like a dinner at any Greek home—and ours being no exception—the door was always open. Most times, Stella joined us since she was best friends with . . . well, all of my sister-in-laws and her brother, Carter, was married to Sophie.

Stella was carrying stuff for my mom, she swept by me and placed it in the middle of the table. I inhaled the scent of her perfume, a mix of spicy and sweet.

"Aunt Stawa," Avril hollered as she waddled over to her.

She scooped down and picked her up. I was mesmerized by their interaction. "If it isn't the one and only evil—I mean, Avril."

16

Her assessment wasn't far off, and I had to cough to cover my laugh.

"Who has the courage to tell her that Avril is just like her?" Carter asked.

"I'm not sure if that's courage, balls, or a death wish," I stated, certainly I wasn't going to be the one to say it. After all, I was getting ready to be with the woman for the next week and needed to play nice if I wanted to survive.

Stella scratched her nose, using her middle finger, of course. Laughing, I stood, offered her my chair, and then headed inside to grab a few more while my brothers moved to dry off little girls, help their wives, or grab the heavier dishes and bring them to the table. When we were all seated, there were seventeen of us not counting Maggie, who was inside sleeping.

Pops, whose only mission in life was to make our mother happy, had all of us help him redo the lanai for her and build —yes, build—her a stone and marble table that curved one side of the pool area. He said that it needed to be big enough to fit our growing families. With wrought iron chairs and bamboo ceiling fans positioned every so many feet along the table, it was probably the best Mother's Day gift she ever got. Even better than the four carat diamond ring he bought her to represent their four kids.

"So, what were you saying about a trip?" Kayson asked after he swallowed his first mouthful of food.

Between bites, I explained about the genetics grant, our goal, and that I was going to a medical conference on the topic. I left off the bit about how I'd requested Stella come with me as my assistant, but told them that the hospital had invited some of the staff who did or used to work in the Women and Children's Unit, and Stella was a part of that.

"So, you're both leaving on Sunday? Are you on the same flight?" Ariel asked.

17

"Yeah, I think so." Okay, that was a lie. I totally knew so since I'd arranged our flights.

"Then why don't I just take both of you together? That will save me from having to take Stella and from Tristan having to arrange a ride as well."

I met Stella's stare and silently asked her if she was willing.

"That's fine, I can drive to your house," Stella offered Ariel.

"Why don't you park at my house? That way your car isn't blocking their driveway." I suggested. It made sense to me.

"Fine, I can park at your house." Stella let out a sigh.

I winked at her, which only made her sigh turn into a snarl. Sometimes, you obeyed the danger warnings, and sometimes, you pulled yourself into a tight ball and jumped.

With Stella, I always tried to cannonball.

I dished out some food before passing the bowl to my right.

"I love this." Mana's voice was full of happiness. "Seeing my boys so happy. Except you, Tristan, when are you going to bring home a sweet girl for me?"

I rolled my eyes, not to my mother, never to my mother. I may be thirty-six, but I wanted to live to see thirty-seven. The woman just didn't understand how exhausting it was for me to have this conversation with her every time we spoke. The woman was relentless. I was pretty sure she knew I liked Stella, so I didn't know why she was making my life so miserable.

"Tristan, answer your mother." Not even Pops was on my side. To him, the only side to be on was his wife's.

"I know, Mana." Not sure which one did it, but one of my brothers kicked me under the table.

"When would that be? Is there anyone special?"

I snapped my head to my right to give the full force of my glare to Damon, who was fighting to hide his smile.

"Don't be so judgmental, maybe he's found a nice young man," Carter added none too helpfully.

I shook my head and tried to block them all out.

Tried being the operative word.

"I have an idea. Greek fest is coming up, so why don't you help me? There are always some nice girls who volunteer. I'll mention you are going to help, that should increase the signup of volunteers as well."

"No, Mana, please don't."

"Why ever not?"

"Yeah, Tristan, why not?" Stella was smirking. That little smirk would drop like a bad habit if I told them that I'd had a one-night stand with her and was waiting for her to figure out that I was the guy she wanted.

"No answer?" Kayson again. He should follow Damon's lead and keep his mouth shut.

"My schedule. Don't volunteer me because I don't know my schedule and with this new genetics grant, I'll be working crazy hours."

"You work too much, no time for fun." Mana let out a huff. "I'll just put you down and then you try."

"Fine, Mana, but I probably won't be able to help. Why not just schedule Kayson, Ian, and Damon, and if I can work a schedule, I can take one of their shifts. Three Christakos boys are always better than one anyway. Plus, there is always Carter." I smiled as I reclined in my seat, feeling a bit satisfied with how I turned it around.

"With Ariel due any day, I can't." Kayson's excuse came first.

"I'm probably on shift," Carter practically shouted.

"With Leo pregnant, I don't want to leave her," Ian defended.

"Maggie is a newborn, I'm helping with so much still," Damon said to Mana, but his focus was on me.

I laughed.

*M*y alarm went off at half past five Sunday morning. I had exactly one hour before I needed to be on the road and headed over to Tristan's.

I reached into my T-shirt drawer and grabbed the first one on top and read it: Get me drunk and enjoy the show. But I decided that I better not, odds were I'd get stuck between some overly religious fanatic or a bratty kid, so I tossed it back into my drawer and pulled out my T-shirt that read: This is not a drill, and had a picture of a hammer on it. I loved watching people slowly get it and then shake their heads. Only disturbed people like me thought it was fucking hysterical.

Then I slipped into jeans and my biker boots, I threw on my makeup, and zipped up my suitcase.

Twenty minutes later, I was turning onto Pente Loop, something about this road sent chills down my spine or maybe it was a sense of longing as in I longed to live here. Hell, my brother and almost all of my friends lived here, so I might as well, too, right? Wrong. Pente Loop was a private road for the Christakos family only, and a Christakos was something that I wasn't.

Driving past the first sprawling house that belonged to Tristan's parents, I curved slightly around the lake and then pulled up the driveway to his home. Since his dad was a custom homebuilder and his older brother, Damon, was an architect, none of the homes were cookie cutter, each was unique and strangely fit each person's personality. Maybe I was being biased, but I loved Tristan's the most, his looked as if someone plucked it right out of the Antebellum era. I expected some Scarlett O'Hara look-alike to walk out the French doors and onto the balcony and invite me in for a mint julep. I laughed at my stupidity, hell, I had no clue what in the fuck a mint julep even was.

I parked and shot Ariel a text to let her know I was there, and when I went to open my door, Tristan was standing there.

"Pop your trunk, I'll get your bags for you."

As I did as he asked, a warm feeling washed over me, something about this whole scene felt very familiar, like . . . Tristan and I were more than colleagues. Maybe it was just my imagination, but hey, if that was the case, then I was going with it.

I didn't get to walk into Tristan's house because Ariel pulled up at that moment, a smile plastered across her face.

"Thanks for picking us up, I know it's early," I said as Tristan opened the car door for me.

"Are you kidding me? I was up anyway, this kid is living on my bladder, and every five minutes I wake up to pee, there is no such thing as a good night's sleep anymore."

"Hey, I'll be right back, I just need to run inside and get my bags and lock up." Tristan gave me a wink and then ran off.

"While he's gone, I have a gift for you." Ariel reached behind her and pulled a small wrapped box from the back seat. Snatching it from her, I went to rip it open, but she stopped me. "No, not now. It's from the girls and me, and it is more of a joke than a gift. It's for when you get to Vegas. Please wait until then. Put it away before Tristan gets back."

If I hadn't been wary before, I would have been after that warning. She was my friend, after all, and as such, anything could be in this box.

"Okay, okay." I held up three fingers and gave a Girl Scout promise even though I was never a fucking Girl Scout. Organized groups were never my thing. Organized crime maybe, but that was probably as far as I went.

The ride to the airport was only about thirty minutes, and Ariel pulled up to the curb in front of the Delta gate at Orlando International Airport.

"Thanks, girl. I'll see you in a week." I went to slide from the car but then turned back to her. "Katy said that she could get me if you can't."

"Nope, I'll be here. It's already on my calendar," Ariel assured me. "You two be good, and find some time to get out of the hotel, play hooky if you have to."

I gave her a hug and then slid from the car before grabbing my backpack as Tristan pulled out luggage from her trunk. Then, with one final wave to Ariel, Tristan and I headed inside to the counter where we checked in our luggage before heading to TSA checkpoint.

With my phone and driver's license out and ready, I headed straight for the TSA checkpoint and got in line. I totally understood why they did this, for fuck's sake, I wanted to fly safely just like the next person, but something about standing in this line made me feel like I was a cow being herded somewhere. Stepping forward, I handed my ID to the agent and scanned my boarding pass, feeling Tristan's warm breath on my neck the entire time.

"Miss, you know that you could have avoided this line and used the Delta Priority line, correct?" The agent pointed several rows over where there was no wait.

"Great, now you tell me."

"You have a first class ticket." He looked at me as though I was stupid.

Okay, dildo, I'm blonde, but that doesn't mean I'm stupid. I snatched my phone from him and looked at my ticket. Holy fuck, I *did* have a first class ticket. "Shit. Sorry. I had no clue that I had a first class ticket. My work bought my ticket and I assumed that I was in a cheap seat."

The TSA agent stared at me, didn't roll his eyes, didn't even crack a smile. No. He was looking at me like . . . well . . . like he didn't give a fuck.

I turned and faced Tristan.

"Is this your doing?"

But before he could answer, the agent was signaling him to step forward. Tristan winked at me and then turned his attention to the agent.

"Sir, you're TSA pre-check, you could go down there."

"I know, but I wanted to be with her."

Tristan pointed at me. The agent turned around and stared. I wasn't sure what he was thinking since he showed no sign of amusement whatsoever.

Once Tristan was through, we made our way to the next section of lines. As I moved slowly through the queue, I ignored the college-aged girls staring at us. By *us*, I meant the sun-kissed Greek demigod next to me, and I didn't blame them. If I could stare without him noticing, I would.

I loaded everything into the plastic buckets and waited for my stuff to disappear into the X-ray machine. When the

TSA officer waved me forward, I stepped into the body scanner and assumed the position, which was that of a homicide victim except instead of lying on the road, I was standing.

Once I was cleared, I went back to waiting, this time for my stuff to come out of the machine. The tub with my iPad was through and so were my shoes, but my backpack was nowhere to be found.

"Whose bag is this?" An agent held up the tan leather sack.

"Mine." I waved and gave Tristan a puzzled look.

"Miss, can you step over here please?" The agent carried my bag to a small station, and I followed him, another officer following. "Can you tell me who packed your bag?"

"I did, why?"

"Has your bag been in your control at all times?"

"Yes. Why?"

"Has anyone asked you to carry anything for them or hold anything for them?"

"No. Will you tell me what the hell is going on?"

The other agent, who was an honest-to-god homeland security officer, reached into my bag and pulled out the small wrapped gift from Ariel. "Miss, what is in this box?"

"I don't know. It's a gift."

"But you said that you packed your bag."

"Exactly, I packed it and put that gift from my friend and sister-in-law into it. It's a gift for me to open when I get to Vegas."

By this time, Tristan had come to stand next to me and was watching the exchange, but he didn't try to intercede.

"Do you mind if we unwrap it here? We have reason to believe that something abnormal is in this package."

"Probably because they are my sisters-in-law and they are

all abnormal," Tristan said in a somewhat low voice. I turned and gave him the evil eye. This was not the time to be funny.

"Open it. I wanted to open it in the car anyway."

The officer walked the package over to the metal device and set it inside. From the looks of it, he was scanning it again. No alarms went off and no one was shouting and trying to arrest me, so clearly, it wasn't a bomb. He must have agreed because he pulled the box out and swabbed it, checking for any trace elements of explosive chemicals. Then, with two other homeland security officers, one flanking each side of him, he unwrapped my fucking gift.

Whatever was inside must have been hilarious, because the big guy in the middle managed to crack a grin. Odds were that whatever they found was payback of some sort, which meant I totally deserved it.

The main officer stepped back, the box being carried gingerly in his outstretched hands as though whatever was inside was going to get him. As he neared me, I turned to stare at Tristan to see if he heard what I heard.

The tunnel shape of the TSA scan area seemed to act as a megaphone, and as the man grew closer, so did the buzzing sound. The officer's face was bright red. "I'm sorry, I couldn't figure out how to turn it off."

"Turn what off?" I stared at him before snatching the gift back and removing the lid. Inside the box was a remote controlled bullet vibrator. On top was a note.

STELLA,
     Don't let Tristan turn you into a bitch, use this instead.
     Love,
     Your Iron Orchids

.   .   .

I GRABBED the remote and pressed the button to turn it off before shoving the entire thing into my backpack. "And this is why we have vibrators. If men can't find the fucking button on this thing when it was clearly labeled, how do we expect you to be able to find the magic button on a woman?"

TRISTAN

*W*hen she met my eyes, I winked. I couldn't help but be impressed by her total lack of embarrassment.

I'd always prided myself on being calm under pressure—hell, I was a doctor, not stressing over little shit was the backbone of my career. But this right here? The thought of Stella, the bane of my existence and the subject of my fantasies, holding a vibrator . . . fuck.

My tie felt extremely tight, so I reached up to loosen it, only to realize that I wasn't wearing a tie. No, I was wearing a plain old button-up with the top button undone. I was dressed to be comfortable for the five-hour flight. Or, I had been before everything started feeling too damn constricting. Before certain images started dancing in my head. Shit, I sounded like a fucking Christmas carol. Christmas . . . present . . . unwrap . . . Stella with a giant bow . . . damn, I needed to get laid. I could no longer focus, one little thought, and I was off on a different tangent.

We still had over an hour, and since I'd personally upgraded us to first class even though there was no way the hospital would reimburse that cost, we had access to the Delta Sky lounge.

The Sky lounge was located on the third floor in the Delta wing, and after showing security our boarding passes, we walked in and found seats in the far corner. There was something to say about flying in style. It was just after seven in the morning and there was already a bartender serving drinks. Dropping our bags off at a small table, we went to grab some food, coffee, and orange juice before making ourselves comfortable, but for the life of me, I couldn't get that damn vibrator out of my mind.

"Did you really not know what was in the package?"

"I had no fucking clue. You know they are going to pay, don't you?"

I nodded. "I'd assume so. What do you have in mind?"

"Oh, it will be good, not sure yet, but I'll let you know when I do."

I stared at Stella, questions I'd wanted to ask her sitting on the tip of my tongue. "Do you ever think about . . ." Stella's face went from happy-go-lucky to I'm going to shove my mug so far up your ass, so I shut up.

She slammed her mug down with a force that had coffee splashing on the glass surface of the small table. "Oh, no you don't, Tristan Christakos, you do not bring that up, not now. We decided that it was best to be forgotten and we've done that for three months. There's no reason to change that."

"Just because it's what is best on paper or in public, it doesn't mean it's what I want. You and I both know what would have happened if the hospital had found out. You'd be looking for a new job. You're their direct employee, I'm only contracted, so they have a lot less control over me."

"And none of that has changed, I'm still an employee."

"But you didn't let me finish, and it seems as if you aren't going to now either."

"Damn right, I'm not. Some things are better left buried, kind of like some people."

"Stella, just listen—"

"No. Not now, not ever."

"You're acting like a four-year-old."

"So?"

The woman was infuriating. Leaning back into the chair, I glanced up at the large screen television that hung on the wall, but if someone were to ask, I wouldn't have been able to tell them what was playing. I was lost in my head, remembering one night three months ago.

I had just closed my office door when a subtle knock had me turning and reopening it. Standing in front of me was the modern-day Marilyn Monroe, blonde hair, blue eyed, and curvy. The woman practically dripped with sexual appeal and had been the leading star of one too many fantasies for years.

From the first time I met her, I wanted to do wicked things to her body, provided she came with duct tape for her mouth. The woman never shut up. I soon realized that she was a voluptuous version of Cinderella with the mouth of a trucker, but she had the heart of Mother Teresa. Although, she didn't like the latter to get out, too afraid it would hurt her tough-girl reputation.

I had needed her that night, and she was there. No, I wasn't crying in a corner, but I was worn out and fucking heartbroken. She must have seen it on my face, seen that I needed a connection to something good, something vibrant, because I took one step and she was in my arms. Her mouth pressed against my lips as she gave and I took.

We were frantic, our hands tangled into each other's clothing, our breathing matching our myriad of emotions. She was still pinned against the wall when she slid down, unzipped the front of my pants, and took me into her mouth.

My medical brain was telling me that it was a mixture of the adrenaline and oxytocin, but something in me knew it was so much more. It was more because somehow we were right for each other. We hadn't admitted it, at least not aloud, but we were.

"Fine. I hate when you're all quiet and grown-up like," Stella said with perfect and terrible timing.

I chuckled. It was just like Stella to not be able to stay angry. "Are you going to let me talk?"

"Not if it is about what happened three months ago."

"But you overreacted," I said and regretted my words once they'd escaped my mouth. The look on her face was a mixture of hurt and anger. "Stella, will you calm the hell down and listen to me?"

"No. No, I will not." She let out a huff. "Besides, I don't overreact."

"Righhhhtt. Just like you didn't three months ago and have never answered my calls since. You still don't know what it was I was actually going to say."

"Who cares? We're friends. That night is long forgotten." Stella dismissed whatever else I was going to say with a flip of her wrist.

I called bullshit; I knew that she was lying. She wouldn't even look at me when she said that last bit. But unlike last time, I didn't want to choke down my words.

"I want you to hear me out."

"About three months ago?"

"Yes."

"Why can't you just let it go?"

Because I didn't want to.

"Fine. I'll make a deal with you." And since I knew her, sometimes better than she knew herself, I added, "Unless, of course, you're chicken."

"Really? That is so amateur. Who calls people chicken

anymore?" Fighting back my grin, I waited. "Now who's acting like a four-year-old?"

I held my tongue, raised one eyebrow, and waited. I should have been counting the seconds.

"Fine, what's the fucking deal?" Stella crossed her arms and flounced back in the seat.

I smiled and then chose my words very carefully, knowing that the idea wasn't really new. No, it had been on my mind since . . . well . . . we went through the TSA check. "Slip into the bathroom and slip that inside." I pointed to her bag.

"What? You want me to wear a bullet vibrator?"

I nodded.

"For how long?"

"Until we get to Vegas."

"What makes you think I would do something like that?"

"Because you never turn down a bet."

She huffed and then looked like she might deny it for all of a minute before she narrowed her eyes at me. "I'm sure you can imagine that having objects up there isn't exactly comfortable unless that object knows what in the fuck it's doing." Stella deadpanned.

"Let me see it."

Stella tossed her backpack over to me, and I rummaged inside and grabbed the remote. "No worries. I know exactly what I'm doing. I'm a doctor after all."

Stella crossed her legs, and I laughed as she squirmed in her seat, pleased that my idea had turned her on. "This is very one sided. What do I get out of it?"

"What do you want?"

"For starters, I want you to never bring up our one-night stand again. No discussing it, anything."

"How about you let me say what I've been trying to tell you, then I promise to never mention it again?"

"Nope, nothing, or deal is off."

I could feel a tic in my jaw increasing because that one request was not good, in fact it pissed me the hell off. "Fine. Then we have a deal?"

Stella let out an evil cackle. "Not even close. You're in a suite in Vegas?"

"Yes."

"I want your room."

"Deal. Anything else?"

"You have to take me to a show while we're there, like one of the Cirque du Soleil shows."

"Fine. Now go into the bathroom." I was still holding her backpack so I pushed it toward her.

She snagged it and headed off. While she was in there, I called the hotel and canceled her room and extended our stay an extra night. She hadn't come out yet, so I pulled up our flight itinerary and moved our return flight from Saturday to Sunday. The confirmation email pinged in my inbox just as she was making her way back to our table.

I pressed the on button.

"Ooo." She let out a gasp and lunged for the remote, but I was faster.

"Oh, no, you don't." I pressed the button again and turned it off.

STELLA

J flexed my body in the spacious leather chair for what had to be the fiftieth time. Thank god, we were in first class, I needed the extra room so I could jab Tristan with my elbow for the same number of times.

"Stop it," I hissed and swiped at his hand, trying to grab the remote from him, but he moved it out of my reach.

"Order another mimosa, you'll be fine."

Through gritted teeth, I mumbled, "I won't be fucking fine because you won't stop playing with that damn remote. Now, give it to me or I'll make your life miserable."

He raised one brow and glared at me.

Oh, I could totally read Tristan's facial expressions. If he thought I was already making his life miserable, he hadn't seen anything yet. Fluffing my blanket out, the thin one that the airline nicely provided but I doubted they washed between flights, I covered Tristan's lap as well as my own. Then curving in toward him, I pretended as though I was going to whisper sweet nothings into his ear and grabbed his nuts instead.

"*Ummph.*"

"That's right, pretty boy, I can control your reproductive organs, too." I gave a light squeeze for effects and then lightly stroked before pulling away. It was cruel, but I liked knowing I could make him hard.

Unfortunately, our entire five-hour flight was nothing more than a game of tit-for-tat. If he pressed the button, then I did something to arouse him. Hell, I'd licked the butter from his croissant off his fingers, making sure to take his fingers in deep. And, of course, my lips, for some strange ass reason were dryer than they'd ever been, so I had to continually lick those as well. Hmmm. Neither of us were letting up or giving in. I was sure the other passengers in first class thought we were auditioning for some porno. The flight attendant had gone as far as to ask if we were on our honeymoon because we seemed to be gaga for each other.

In truth, though, it was all a facade. Maybe it was a facade. Okay, I was telling myself it was a facade. If I told myself often enough, then I'd believe it . . . right?

I curled up into my seat and rested my head against the window while Tristan typed away on his laptop.

"What are you doing?"

"Just researching some new medications that reps have been trying to get the hospital to use."

"Oh." I yawned and curled a little tighter, totally forgetting about the funky-ass vibrator.

The taxi ride from the airport to the Venetian was quick, and walking in was like stepping into another world with the fresco ceilings and gothic archways. Shifting my weight from leg to leg as we stood in line at the check-in, I couldn't get my mind off one thing . . . a nice cold shower . . . away from Tristan. If I was going to do as he had wanted and pretend nothing had happened between us, then I needed to cool my libido. Oh, I was seriously wondering if this damn bullet was waterproof.

"Next." The registration clerk waved us forward. "How may I help you?"

"Checking in for Christakos, C-H-R-I—"

"Yes, I have you right here, Mr. Christakos. We have you in our Prima suite for seven nights."

I'd been standing to the side and just listening to Tristan, but the clerk's words caught me off guard. "Seven?" I asked.

"Yes, seven."

Maybe Tristan was staying after I left. Something about that was disheartening because I kind of liked traveling with him. I liked the time we'd been together, in fact, it was what I'd always wanted. He was the perfect man in so many ways. Well, at least he was the perfect man for me, and that was all I'd ever cared about. I just hated that I couldn't have him.

"Here are your keys and a map. The elevators are over there." The clerk pointed behind us and to our right. "If you need anything, there is a concierge on your floor."

"Thank you." Tristan turned, a smile wide on his face. Something in his look gave me an ominous feeling. "You ready? The bellman will bring our bags up."

"How will they know which bags go where?"

"Our luggage tags have our names on them, so they'll just bring them up." Tristan placed one hand at the base of my back and the gesture made my back arch, my posture curve as I moved closer to him a little more. He escorted me to the bank of elevators then walking on, he pressed number eighteen.

"We're both on the same floor?"

"Yep."

When the doors opened, we exited and I followed him. "What rooms are we looking for?"

"This one," Tristan said, stopping in front of room 1818. He swiped the key in front of the door and pushed it open.

"Holy fuck." I was in awe. "This is bigger than my townhome." I moved into the room and set my purse on a table, then headed straight to the bathroom. It was time for the bullet and me to go our separate ways.

When I exited the large marble bathroom, I moved to the giant picture window that overlooked the strip and took in Treasure Island, which was across the street. "I feel guilty for taking this from you."

Tristan didn't get to answer because there was a knock at our door, and he opened it to let the bellman in. "Where would you like me to set the luggage?"

"On the bed is fine," Tristan said and then pulled out his wallet and grabbed a bill for a tip. The bellman left as quickly as he'd entered.

I moved to start putting my clothes away, wanting to get my skirts hanging to help with wrinkles. "Where's your room?"

"Here."

"Whoa. What?"

"You said you wanted my room and that I had to take you to a show. You're in my room and I'll take you to a show. I cancelled the other room."

He had the nerve to smile. "I used to think that your brown eyes were sexy."

"Used to?"

"Yep. Used to. Now they just remind me that you are full of shit. You knew what I meant and you completely distorted —wait . . . this is a king room only. Tell me that couch pulls out to a bed." I yanked the cushions from the couch, but there was no bed. "Call the front desk and ask for a roll-away."

"Stella, stop. You are what, five-ten? I'm six-two, you and I both know that neither of us will fit on a roll-away."

"Then call the front desk and see if there's another room available."

"No."

"Fine, then I will." I stepped forward and Tristan grabbed my wrist before pulling me against him, his face mere inches from mine.

"What's the problem? You said that our time together three months ago meant nothing, so what's the big deal if we share the bed? It's a California King."

"Propriety."

Tristan laughed. Not a chuckle, either. He flat-out laughed as though what I'd said was the fucking funniest thing he'd ever heard.

"Fuck you. Regardless, we aren't sleeping together."

"Fine, we won't sleep together. If I recall, we couldn't have done much sleeping last time either."

"Stop that," I demanded. "You aren't funny."

Tristan lowered his mouth next to my ear and placed several quick kisses just below my lobe. "Whatever you say, boss."

"If I'm the boss, then where are you sleeping?"

"In the bed."

"Then where am I sleeping?"

"In the bed."

"Tristan, this isn't funny." He began placing those damn fucking kisses again. "Fine. But I may fart during the night, and we aren't having sex." I marched off and finished unloading my suitcase. By the time we were done, it was past lunch, and I was starving.

Tristan was either on the same page as I was or he knew me too well because he asked, "Want to go down and find something to eat or chill up here and order room service?"

"Let's go explore." I snagged my purse and headed for the door. "Oh, can I have a key just in case we get separated?"

"Sure, but we won't." Tristan gave me a key and then followed me back out.

Once on the elevator, he slipped his hand into mine, I pulled away.

Lunch was a battle of wills to see who could flirt the most without drawing attention, which we failed spectacularly at, but we made it through without being kicked out.

"Wait, Tristan," I said, tugging him away from the elevators when he was trying to tug me to them, "don't we need to go check-in for the conference?" The conference was being held at the Sands Convention Center, which was connected to The Venetian. I had never quite understood why so many medical conferences were held in Las Vegas until I got to truly know Tristan. If all doctors were like him, then we had some seriously skilled sex-perts in the world.

"Hush," he whispered, but his words were still a forceful command.

"Don't tell me to hush." But there was no anger in my voice.

His fingers lightly tightened as he pressed the number eighteen on the elevator when the doors closed, and I realized that no one else was inside. Tristan reached around the front of me and pulled me back against him, his palm cupping one breast. His hard erection pressed into my back. When the doors opened, Tristan was frantic. Like a starved man being shown a feast, he was racing forward and dragging me with him. He couldn't get the key out of his pocket fast enough or the door to our room open quickly enough. When finally we were inside and the door slammed shut, I heard the *cling* of metal on tile, and it took me only half a second to realize what it was. That was the sound of metal—Tristan's metal buckle, to be exact—hitting the tile of the floor as Tristan dropped his belt to the floor. He reached forward, lifted the hem of my shirt over my head and then lowered his head to my breast and eased the lacy fabric of my bra away until he could take one nipple into his mouth.

"Oh, god."

"Not god, Tristan. Just call me Tristan."

"Ass, I'm going to call you ass."

Before I could protest, or pretend to protest, he'd swept me up into his arms and was carrying me toward the bedroom.

Tristan kissed me as he walked, and I soaked in all that was this Greek god that I'd secretly fallen in love with over the last few years. He was everything that a man should be . . . funny, kind, considerate, and as I had discovered a few months ago an incredible lover.

Closing my eyes, I inhaled the smell of vetiver, a scent that would forever trigger images of Tristan. It was warm and earthy, yet still possessed an exotic mystery.

My eyes fluttered shut as he kissed me, drawing my lip between his teeth before he deepened our kiss, swirling his tongue around mine. I let out a tiny moan of pleasure as he laid me onto the bed and stretched my arms above my head. His arousal pressed against my leg, and pleasure pulsed through me knowing that I had as much of an effect on him as he had on me. He never broke contact with my lips, and the sweet sensation of his mouth and his tongue against mine mixed with the pressure of his body against me had my passion at an all time high.

I was on the verge of exploding with the need to be touched. My body was responding to his, and although I knew he could wake up tomorrow and tell me that what we shared was nothing but passion, there was nothing that would stop me from going through with this. I was one hundred percent surrendering my body to him.

He released his hold on my hands so he could cup both breasts, and I let my fingers sink into his hair. Lightly tugging from the base of his scalp, I enjoyed the feel of shivers that seemed to vibrate through his body with each pull. Finally turning my attention to his muscular and taut shoulder and arms, I massaged them before sliding down even farther to his hips. He broke our kiss so he could skim his lips over my neck.

"You're so beautiful, so fucking beautiful," Tristan crooned.

Brushing his fingers along the line of my jaw and tracing it to the bottom of my ear, he set my skin on fire. I didn't have the power to push him away from me, nor did I have the will. I had nothing in me but need . . . raw, pulsing, need.

He scooted back so his hands were wrapped around my ankles. Sliding up my calves to my denim-clad thighs, he massaged the delicate skin upward until he reached the space between my legs. Moving up just a tiny bit more, he unsnapped my jeans and slid them off, tossing them to the floor with the rest of our discarded clothes and shoes. All that was left were Tristan's jeans.

When his fingers found my center, I let out a deep moan of approval. The man had magical fucking hands.

He groaned with pleasure when I trailed my fingers down his back and around his hips until I was yanking at the button on his jeans. Pulling himself up, he quickly stripped out of his jeans and then rejoined me.

He lifted his head as if he meant to say something, but he didn't speak at first. He only stared at me.

Taking what I'd wanted and been dreaming about one too many nights, I moved toward his stiff cock and began to stroke him. At that moment, it didn't matter whether it was science or religious belief, there was one thing I knew for certain and that was the Big Bang theory was real because I was getting ready to see it in real life. Tristan's head was thrown back, his chest pushed forward as I stroked up and down, and tiny chills rippled across his nerves as he fought the urge to explode. When the first beads of precum beaded on the tip, I met his eyes as I licked my lips and then moved toward it, but he pressed one hand on my head stopping me.

"Stella."

When he whispered my name with such raw desire, it only intensified my need for him.

"Wait. Give me a second."

I fought back the urge to smirk. Sometimes, it was nice to be reminded who held the power.

"No," Tristan amended. "We have all day and night."

Strangely, it was a turn-on being ordered about. So, instead of continuing my need to make him cum, I spent several seconds admiring his magnificent body, a body any sculptor would love to get their hands on. I kissed his chest, my tongue on his nipples before moving ever so slowly and flitting over his body.

He slid one hand between my legs. "I want to feel you and taste every inch of you."

"What a coincidence, I want the exact same things." With my words, he had me on my back, and he was straddling me, one of his legs settling between my thighs as I arched against him, trying to get closer. He covered my breasts with his palms and gently massaged them. The hard nubs of my nipples pressed upward, pleading to be squeezed. I bit my lip as I silently begged him to hurry up, to get inside me.

"I need you. I want you inside me."

Tristan was working at his own speed, and slowly, he spread my legs wide open, leaned in, and licked my slit, raking his tongue up and down my pussy.

With each swipe of his tongue, a rapid fire of pleasure blasted through my body, and my stomach rippled as I flexed up to meet him.

"Holy fuck," I cried out as my orgasm built to climax.

Abruptly, he withdrew his tongue, cutting my orgasm short.

"Nooo," I cried.

"No, what?"

"Don't stop, I want more."

Tristan had the fucking nerve to chuckle. I sat up, but he lightly pushed on my chest and had me falling back onto the bed.

"No, Tristan, really."

"Just wait, Stella. We aren't in a hurry."

"You may not be, but I sure as fuck am. Now, get inside me."

The rumble from his laugh vibrated against my abdomen where he rested his chin to look up at me. I felt him squeeze my hips, and that single gesture had me opening my legs and my lips in sync. He crawled up my body until he was able to gently take my lower lip between his teeth and then ran his tongue just inside my mouth till they entwined. We stayed this way, tongues exploring, fingers trailing up and down each other's bodies, for a few long minutes before he pulled away. Slowly, he kissed his way down my whole body, but his tongue lingered over and around my aching nipples while I writhed beneath him.

It wasn't long before his tongue was laving over me, tracing long slow circles around my clit. I buried my hands into his hair and held his head against me as I writhed my hips in rhythm with his tongue. I could feel it building . . . the release that I'd been longing for . . . faster and stronger. He took my swollen clit between his lips and sucked . . .

"Oh, god, Tristan, I'm coming. Fuckkkk." I let go of his hair and threw my arms back, bucking my hips repeatedly as he held me tight and relentlessly assaulted me with his tongue. My body shook and convulsed until I was limp. Once he felt my body ease, he gently crawled on top of me and kissed me deeply, running his lips all over mine. I could taste myself on him . . . it was salty and musky . . . and fucking erotic.

Tristan curled up against me but made no attempt to make love to me. My mind was hazy, but I knew this wasn't right, not the norm. "What about you?"

"What about me?"

"What about your pleasure?"

"I just had my pleasure."

"You came?" I asked, his words making no sense to me as I tried to clear away the sex filled cobwebs.

"No. My pleasure was doing that to you."

I curled in closer to him, I'll think about what he just said later. I closed my eyes, comfortable in his arms.

TRISTAN

*S*tella was still sound asleep after her orgasm, and I mentally patted myself on the back for that one as I checked the clock. Registration and cocktails were at six, fuck, we had about an hour to get ready.

"Hey, love, it's time to wake up." I loved the way her long blonde hair splayed out around the pillow.

"Do I have to?" She arched her back to stretch, and it forced her ass against my cock, my extremely sore cock.

My cock that wanted . . . no, begged for release. Why the hell did I have to be so gallant and romantic and tell her that I was there for her pleasure? Who did I think I was, fucking Casanova? No. I needed relief, and if she kept wiggling her body, she was going to experience my relief.

Settling one hand on her hip, I held her steady. "Let's not do that, or we will miss registration."

Stella let out a devious cackle and then buried her head under the sheets. "My, oh, my, what do we have here?"

"Stella, stop."

"Why? It looks like someone wants to come out and play." She grabbed hold and squeezed my hard cock as she slid her tongue over me. I could only see the motion of the sheet as her head bobbed, but just knowing that it was this woman who I'd had one too many dreams about had the pressure already building inside me. When my tip hit the back of her throat, I rocked forward, begging her to take more. She did, and my head fell back against the pillows as she had her way with me. Still, I wanted to see her, so I tucked the sheet away and watched as her mouth and tongue moved over me. As her hand wrapped around the base of my cock.

It started at the base of my spine, this rolling build-up of tension that was somewhere between pain and the sweetest pleasure.

"Baby, I'm getting ready to cum." My words only set her on a frenzy of suction as she twirled her tongue in a myriad of motions.

The rolling thunder in my body erupted, and the velvet edge of Stella's tongue swiped back and forth as she cleaned me up. Her vibrant blue eyes locked with mine the entire time.

This, this was definitely something I wanted every day and night.

A FEW MINUTES AFTER SIX, Stella and I walked off the elevator and into the reception area for conference attendees.

"So exactly what am I supposed to be doing?" Stella waved one wrist in the air as though she didn't really care what my answer was going to be.

"I want to turn my focus as a neonatologist to one who specializes in genetic birth defects. I put your name in to be my nursing assistant on this project. Once it is up and running, there will be a promotion for you, Mrs. Cameron promised me that."

"You asked for me to have a promotion?"

"Of course. I mean, come on, you're going to be stuck with me after all."

"Oh, the horror." Stella bumped my shoulder.

"Tristan, is that you?" I looked up to see who had cut off my conversation with Stella and smiled. I knew the woman but couldn't remember how I knew her.

"Yes, it's me." Shit, what was her name?

"You have no clue who she is, do you?" Stella whispered.

I glanced over my shoulder to give Stella and her not-needed commentary a silent, *your help is not fucking needed right now.* But she only smiled wider and winked.

"You're still just as gorgeous. Are you here for the conference?"

"We are. It was last minute, but I'm interested to see what they are presenting."

"So, you're into genetics research now? Is this for neonatal, or have you switched?"

"My, doesn't she know a lot about you? Stalker much?" Stella whispered, and I fought to hold back my groan.

"I've been working to add a genetics research lab to the hospital where I work in hopes of helping with hereditary birth defects and infant donor matches."

"You always were so giving," the woman, whose name I still hadn't remembered, said.

"Well, let me tell you what he gave me earlier today."

I coughed at Stella's words.

"Are you okay?" The woman reached forward and placed a hand on my arm. "Wow, you're built, aren't you?"

I slid out of her reach. "Have you registered yet? I still need to do that."

"Yep, just did." She waved a folder in front of me.

Really? If she was registered, then why in the hell had she not put her name badge on? They were there for a reason.

"How's everything been going in Orlando? You're still at Orlando Regional?"

Okay, this woman knew way too much about me for me to not even remember her. "Everything is going great. Excited that we are adding a genetics center. How about at your . . . hospital?"

"Crazy as ever, but I spend a lot more time in a lab than you do. How is your family? You have three brothers, right?"

I gave Stella a quick glance and could tell that she was fighting to hold back her laugh or some smartass comment. This woman had just crossed over and had my stalker warnings going off. "Yep, three, and all three are married now."

"But you are still single?"

Taking a step back, I avoided her question because I was totally uncomfortable with how much this woman knew about me and how intrusive she was and then turned to Stella. "Stella, are you ready to go register?"

"Absolutely." Stella flicked her hair and then gave me a devious smile, I inwardly groaned, knowing that the woman was capable of anything. "Hi, I'm Stella Lang." Stella held out her hand to introduce herself.

"Oh, I'm sorry. I'm Elyse Gordon, I'm a geneticist at Mercy Hospital in Miami."

"Elyse, that's it." Both women turned to stare at me.

"Did you say something?" Elyse asked.

"No, nothing. It was nice seeing you again, Elyse, I better get registered."

"Perhaps we can have drinks later, just you and me?" She glanced over at Stella, who was back to trying hard not to laugh. The one thing I had to say about Stella was that she wasn't the jealous sort. And something in me hated that; I wished that she were jealous.

Stella smiled at me and winked. "That sounds lovely. I'm

sure I can find something, or someone, to keep me entertained."

Oh, hell no. "Thanks, Elyse, but Stella is actually my girlfriend." Stella looked startled by me calling her my girlfriend, but really, what did she expect after her little comment?

"I'm so sorry, I didn't know." Elyse looked embarrassed, which wasn't my intention, but she did put me on the spot. Plus, I'd be damned if I was going to let Stella out of my sight for one second in a place known as sin city.

"It's okay. We are keeping it quiet and professional while we are here."

I settled my hand on the small of her back and urged Stella toward the registration area. Leaning over, I whispered into her ear, "Not funny, not fucking funny at all."

Stella shrugged. "What?"

"You know what? There won't be any other men to keep you entertained. Just like there won't be any other women for me."

"Hmmm. Boyfriend and girlfriend? How fifth grade of us. I don't remember you passing me a note on the playground."

"I didn't, I gave you an oral report, remember?" My words got to her and sent a shiver ricocheting through her body.

I love feeling her wiggle.

DAY ONE OF THE CONFERENCE . . . was boring. Granted, I found the advancement in genetic research fascinating, and the decrease in infant mortality rate due to determine the pre-disposition to genetic defect as astounding.

I was taking notes and thought that Stella was taking notes on her iPad as well, until I saw something red fly across the screen.

"What are you doing?" I whispered.

"Playing Angry Birds."

"Why aren't you listening to this?"

"It's boring."

I met her eyes and smiled. "Let's go." I tilted my head toward the back of the room. She left, and a minute later, I followed. On my way out, a few doctors glanced my way, all of whom probably knowing exactly where I was going.

Twenty minutes later, Stella and I were standing at the top of New York, New York, and she was bouncing like a kid in a candy store.

"Next," the young man hollered, and we climbed onto the Big Apple roller coaster cart. It was designed to look like a yellow taxicab.

"You ready?"

"Hell, yes, bring it." Stella let out a cackle.

I wrapped my hands through the metal grip as the cart started to move. The sounds of horns honking filled the air as the car jerked, stopped, and simulated Manhattan traffic. When it picked up speed for the upcoming loop, Stella shouted.

"Let go of the bar and lift your feet off the ground." Stella held out her left hand and grabbed ahold of mine and held them out in front of us. Then she pulled her knees up just as we approached the base of the loop, and I followed.

When we entered the inversion, I pressed my feet to the bottom of the cart because, fuck no, I was coming out of my seat.

The coaster dipped and curved off the top of the hotel so we could see miles of the Las Vegas strip stretched out around us. It was all of two minutes later that the car was pulling back into the hotel and my stomach was a little queasy.

"Okay, am I getting old . . . don't answer that, or was the ride that choppy?" I held my stomach.

"Both. Come on." Stella tugged my hand and pulled me to another window.

"What's this?" I read the sign and smiled. "Cirque du Soleil, Zumanity. Is this the show that you want?" Stella had a smile on her face, which made me a little nervous, but I handed my card over to the ticket agent. "Two adults please."

"For which evening?"

"This week, whichever night you have the best seats." The teller clicked on her computer a few minutes. "I have two seats in the center on the lower level for Thursday night's show if you'd like them."

"Perfect. We'll take those."

"Are you familiar with Zumanity?"

"No. She wants to see it." I turned and pointed at Stella, who was trying to hide the fact that she'd just had her finger in front of her mouth. "What are you hiding? Who are trying to hush?" I stared at her, but she didn't answer, not that I thought she would. Stella gave me a sweet and innocent look and then reached forward and grabbed the tickets.

"Thank you. He and I will have so much fun." She winked at the woman behind the counter.

"Thank you."

"For what? Holding the tickets?"

"No. For agreeing to come. I like having you here. You seem different."

"You mean *we* seem different?"

"Maybe that's it, I don't know."

"At home we always have the structure of work. You're a doctor, and I'm a nurse. At home, your mother is trying to fix you up. I think here we can just be us."

"I think that Mana is trying to see if you'll react when she mentions fixing me up, don't you ever watch her?"

"No, should I?"

"She always keeps her eyes on you. I think she knows

53

something." I pulled Stella closer to me. This week, I had one week to show her what she wouldn't allow me to say the morning after our one-night stand.

DAY TWO OF THE CONFERENCE . . . was a waste, a fucking waste.

All I could remember was that Stella wore a navy-blue pencil skirt with a light-blue shirt. And, somehow, the whole outfit seemed to hug every inch of her body. I couldn't keep my eyes off her.

"What are you staring at, Doctor?"

"You."

"You should be paying attention to the presentation."

I tried, I really did, when the presenter mentioned a bone marrow registry, I tried to turn my focus away from the modern day pin-up model, but it was no use. One fact remained: five o'clock couldn't get here fast enough.

When the conference day was over and we finally hit our room, all deals about keeping it professional were off and our clothes were thrown haphazardly between the door and the bed. We couldn't get undressed fast enough.

At this rate, my conscience wasn't going to allow me to claim any part of this trip as a business expense. Nope, the guilt was heavy because there was little business getting done. It was supposed to be a work trip but it had turned into a sex-a-thon with breaks for work.

When Stella got out of the shower, she sat on the bed next to me and ran a brush through her hair as I leaned against the headboard, flipping through channels.

"Your hair looks so much longer."

"It's just 'cause it's wet."

I took the brush from her. "I've never brushed a woman's hair." Stella crawled over me so she was nestled between my legs, and I pulled the bristles through her blonde tresses.

"You still haven't picked out a movie yet?"

"Was waiting on you."

"I'm easy, I like everything."

"Scary?"

"Bring it, Chainsaw Massacre, Freddy, The Kardashians."

"Kardashians?"

"Yeah, those are some scary ass bitches, ever see those women ugly cry?"

I continued brushing. There was something soothing and erotic about what I was doing. It was stupid, I knew it was, but I felt closer to her than I ever had before. "What's your favorite movie?"

"Vacation or Christmas Vacation."

"Really? Not some chick flick?"

"Yes, really. Have you seen them? They are hysterical. You know Jane Krakowski is the hick cousin in the original movie, I about die when she asks about French kissing then says with a straight face that her daddy says that she is the best. There are so many lines like that. It's genius, I tell you, pure genius." Stella was thoroughly enjoying her exaggeration. "In Christmas Vacation when Cousin Eddie shows up with his RV and everyone is standing around outside looking at the lights. They invite the kids to stay in the house so Eddie and his wife can have some alone time, I make everyone shut the hell up just so I can hear him say the line about the rubber sheets and gerbils."

"What? He doesn't say anything like that."

"Cross my heart, he does."

"We are so watching them, I'll have to find them on my iPad. I always thought the funniest line was, 'Shitter's full.'"

"They changed something for European and Vegas Vacations, they weren't nearly as funny."

"Agreed. Here we are in Vegas, and I can't remember anything about that movie except when they play Keno."

"I know, right?" Stella leaned forward and took the brush back from me. "Thank you. I liked having you do that."

"I liked it, too, in fact, I like just being with you." I grabbed her arm and pulled her back down to me so our foreheads were touching. "Now's your chance. If this, us, seeing what we can be isn't what you want, tell me now." I held my breath, waiting for her to say something, and when she didn't, I let out a sigh and then brought her mouth to mine.

DAY THREE OF THE CONFERENCE . . .

Understanding how genetic panels worked and then coming to the understanding that even with all of the advancements in medicine that it still took around four weeks to get a complete autosomal panel comparison back was astounding.

If we could get a man on the moon faster than we could get DNA read, something in our government funds was seriously lacking. Granted, it was the most thorough DNA test available and it examined the sixteen different markers, but four weeks was a long time.

After the conference, I took Stella to dinner at Gordon Ramsey Steak. I figured if any chef was her soul mate, it had to be him. Two people who cussed like truckers, gave their opinions whether you wanted them or not, and somehow still made people love them—I froze at that last bit . . . love. Had I fallen in love with Stella? Love was too strong of a word, wasn't it? I mean, we'd just had dinner for christ's sake. But…she has been a significant part of my life for the past several years. And truth be told, I couldn't imagine not having her in my life. Love? Hmmm, I'll have to think on that later when I wasn't staring into her vibrant blue eyes.

After our dinner, we walked to the Eiffel Tower. "Have you been to Vegas before?"

"Do you remember when Las Vegas was going for the whole family feel? They were trying to rebrand themselves as a family destination, so they'd cleaned up the streets and started to put out ads that made it seem almost wholesome?"

Something about that seemed like an oxymoron since Vegas was more like a synonym for wild drunken parties and medical conferences. "I remember something about it."

"Yeah, it was the mid-nineties. Anyway, my mom and one of her husbands—"

"Whoa, one of her husbands? How many has she had?"

"Four."

"You don't talk about her much."

"We aren't real close. Anyway, as I was saying, she brought Carter and me to Vegas, we stayed at Circus, Circus, and Mom got Carter and me our own room. There was an entire amusement park inside the hotel, and he and I basically spent the whole time running through the place unsupervised. I totally blame Circus Circus for my addiction to Krispy Kreme donuts."

"Why?"

"They had a bakery right inside the hotel, and when we walked through to the main part, you could smell them. If the red light was on, it meant that the donuts were on the conveyor belt running under the glaze at that moment. There's nothing better than tasting that warm, sweet, delicate—"

"I get the picture." I stopped Stella since I did indeed get the picture but the only problem was, I was envisioning something totally different that was sweet, warm, and delicate.

"What about you? How many times have you been here?"

Stella asked as we left the Parisian and headed out to the strip.

"I've been here a bunch of times, but this is the first time I've gotten to explore. It's kind of cool, like Disney World for adults."

"Look, there's Dumbo." Stella pointed to some idiot walking down the middle of the road with cars honking, trying to get him to move.

"I bet that's Snow White." I gave a slight chin nod to a woman standing on the corner. There were several guys around her. "She even has Grumpy, Dopey, and Doc with her."

We walked a little bit more while she swung our clasped hands back and forth as if we were kids. "Where did the Christakos go for vacations?"

"Usually abroad. Mana always wanted to go home and visit her family. She has a lot of brothers, and they all still live in Greece. I mean, we have cousins who have moved here, but her family owns a shipyard. Our family vacations always revolved around trips to Greece, we'd stop other places, but they were usually in Europe."

"Must be nice. I saw places that my mom wanted to see, and we went to Chicago, New York, and California, but only if it was something she wanted. I think that's why Carter and I are so close. She always had stuff to do, and we were always left to entertain ourselves."

"If you could go anywhere, where would it be?"

"I'd like to see Greece. I've sort of fallen in love with your family and your mother's cooking—"

I stopped in the middle of the sidewalk and pulled Stella into my arms. "Just my family?"

"Just your family, what?" She gave me a devious grin. She totally knew what it was I was fishing for. "You have to admit it, your brothers are pretty hot."

"You'll regret that."

"Promise?" Stella bit her lower lip, but she wasn't trying to act innocent. No, she was going for temptress and she was playing it very well.

Our stroll along the strip had relaxed us and all I wanted to do was to get back and spend the evening with her, trying to get her to confess that she was in love with me, too.

DAY FOUR OF THE CONFERENCE . . .

Stella was different in Vegas. Sure she was still sarcastic and funny as well as drop-dead sexy but there was a passion in her that I'd never seen before. I hated being away from her even for a few moments. When she snuck out of the conference because the medical talk got too technical, I felt her absence . . . like, I wasn't all there either. It was weird.

Just before lunch, Stella returned because the attendees were going to be their first test subjects. To show the comparison, we would actually be set against our partners. We went into the makeshift lab area where the technicians drew our blood and collected hair samples. My and Stella's samples were packaged together for comparison. The idea was to show how you could find matches from universal and non-universal donors.

After we were done, Stella and I took a look at what was next on the itinerary—Equipment Display—and turned for the exit. Since our hospital was just beginning the process of building this program, looking at equipment wasn't high on my priority list.

Back in the room, Stella snagged the two tickets for the show tonight and shoved them into her pocket. "I'm so excited. I wanted to see this one or O."

"There's more than one?"

"Yes, there's like seven." She rolled her eyes at me as if this was something that everyone knew, everyone but me.

"How was I supposed to know?"

"O is all done in water . . . imagine the best aerialists who are also cliff divers. Then there are synchronized swimmers, it's amazing."

"It sounds like you've seen that one."

"Nope, just researched it on YouTube."

"Then what is Zumanity about?"

Stella tapped one perfectly polished nail against her lips and gave me a wicked smile. "I have no idea."

"Why do I think that you're lying to me?"

She laughed while I resisted the urge to pull it up on my phone.

Thirty minutes later, we were sitting in the back of the boat as a gondolier pushed us around the recreation of Piazza San Marco. Much like its namesake in Venice, high-end stores lined the walkway.

"This is kinda romantic, isn't it?" Stella whispered.

"Yeah. Kinda," I whispered back, but truth was, it was a whole lot of romantic.

"In all your travels, have you been to Venice?"

"Yeah, Italy is a short flight from Greece or you can take the ferry."

"I'm so jealous."

Tucking a stray hair behind her ear, I said, "I'll take you, I promise." I wanted to take her to see the world more than anything else at that very moment. Okay, that sounded cheesy, but this woman with all her tough edges and I-don't-care attitude made me want to . . . well . . . she made me want to take care of her. Although, I knew she'd fight me every step of the way, it sure would be fun trying.

"Mana wanted to see Venice and take a gondola ride so we went to Venice and took a boat ride."

"That's all it takes? Mana wants it?"

"Pops' whole life has revolved around making my mother happy." I'd never really reflected back on what all my father did for her, but as much as her mission was to take care of us kids and Pops, his was to pamper her. I wanted to do that for a woman...for Stella.

"She doesn't seem like a hard person to make happy."

"Funny thing is, she isn't. She just wants all of us happy. But I think that is why she is always trying to fix me up with someone. She really doesn't believe anyone can be happy single since she is so happy being married."

"Are you happy?"

"I thought I was."

"You thought? But what, you realized you weren't?"

"I realized that I could be happier."

"Oh."

I leaned forward and swept my mouth over hers, tasting the mixture of dessert and her lip gloss. "How about you, are you happy?"

"I am right now."

Just before seven, Stella and I walked back over to the New York hotel and casino. With my hand resting at the base of her back, I found myself standing a little taller just knowing that this gorgeous woman was next to me.

"I've been to Venice and our hotel is a great rendition, but except for running through JFK, I've never been to New York. How did they do capturing the life of the city?" I asked.

"Honestly, nothing can capture New York. I hate crowds, but in New York, I seem to forget it. It's almost as if the noise turns into a part of the backdrop. You are surrounded by these huge skyscrapers, and you know that amazing things are happening inside them. Whether it's some billion-dollar deal or some famous person boinking his secretary that soon will be exploited all over the tabloids. Whatever is happening in New York will trickle down to the rest of the United States, and we eat it up."

"That sounds overwhelming."

"It is, but Orlando can be that way, too."

"Just not on the same scale, right?"

"Exactly." She grinned at me, pleased that I understood what she was saying. "I haven't been to New York in years, though. So, there is a chance I wouldn't feel that way about it anymore."

"When was the last time you visited?"

Stella took a second to think about it, and I kind of wanted to brush my thumb over the small crease that formed between her eyebrows.

"I think I was fourteen."

"Did you and Carter go with just your mom or both parents?"

"My parents split when I was six, so we went with just our mom. She was dating some guy at the time, and we'd fly out there when he had meetings and she wanted to see him."

"That sounds . . ."

"Boring? It was, but I loved New York. It's just that my vacations were nothing like yours. I love her, don't get me wrong, she's my mom, after all, and she's never been cruel to me. She just isn't what anyone wouldn't pick out as a mom if you were flipping through a catalog. She really should have stayed single and childless all her life."

I'd known most of this already from her brother, Carter, his kids had two sets of grandparents, Sophie's mom and my parents; his parents were nowhere in the mix, but hearing her say it so matter-of-factly threw me for a second. Not the statement in and of itself, but the almost clinical nature of it. As if Stella knew her mother was who she was and didn't want to judge her or spend her whole adult life being bitter because her mother wasn't . . . motherly.

"I've never had a desire to go to New York, but you make me want to visit. How about Broadway? Did you see any shows?"

"Never been but would love to. You know there are Broadway shows that come to Orlando, right? We have that huge Broadway center that Disney built. They get all the shows. I've been to a few but keep promising myself to look up the schedule and try to go to more."

"When we get home, you should look up season passes so we can go."

"Really? You'd go?"

"Sure I would. I appreciate stuff like that. Actors have to learn a few lines, but Broadway performers have to learn their lines, learn their songs, and learn their dance routines. That isn't counting making sure that it is in step with everyone else. Give credit where credit's due."

We headed into the theater and were shown to our seats, when the lights went out and the show began, I was mesmerized and then I was somewhat embarrassed. Of course, that was before I remembered we were in Vegas and anything goes.

"Holy shit, is this the porno Cirque?"

"Shhh," Stella hissed. She wrapped one arm around mine and curled against me as we watched two women in what could only be described as a water bowl as they glided and slid in the most erotic moves as they continually came face-to-face with each other. Their bodies were scantily clad, and holy shit, I was turned on.

Stella must have been equally as turned on because tiny goose bumps were exploding across her arms every time I brushed against her. When I trailed my index finger across one perk nipple, her whole body quivered. Yep, she wanted me, too.

I was a goner. I was lost for this woman.

TRISTAN

*D*ay five of the conference . . .

     By the time the conference was over, I knew that the hospital investing in a genetics testing facility was important, but I also knew that getting out of there and back up to our room was even more important.

"We've been playing this game for two years," I said as soon as the door closed behind us. She was in front of me, her back pressed to my front as I dropped soft kisses along her shoulder.

"What game?"

"Keep away, where we tried to keep away from each other. But I can't, not anymore. I want you. I have you, and I don't want another day without you."

"I didn't think you even saw me. All this time, I thought that I was more of a nuisance."

"I saw you, I fucking saw every inch of you, inside and out." I blew warm air along the curve of her neck until she was pressing back against me and tilting her head even more to give me better access.

"Your perfect lips." I trailed one finger along the seam until her mouth parted.

"Your generous heart that you try to hide even though it always comes out whether you want it to or not." I felt her heart race, a rhythm that felt like a secret code that only I could decipher.

Stella pulled away and turned just enough so she could stick her tongue out at me. I laughed and stalked her deeper into the suite.

"In fact, I think I've been falling for you these last two years. Kayson and Damon fell fast, but I think I'm more like Ian." Okay, bringing my brothers up at a time like this may not be the most romantic thing, but I had to explain what I was feeling, and I didn't know what else to say.

My arms were aching to reach forward and pull her closer, but something in me told me to tread lightly. She wasn't acting like I thought she would, not that I'd imagined this moment or anything. But . . . I just didn't imagine her covering her face and pulling away from me. "Don't, Stella." I cupped her face and tilted her head back. "Please, let me see your beautiful blue eyes." How had I misjudged her feelings so completely?

Grabbing hold of her wrists, I gently urged her to drop her hands. "What's wrong? Why are you crying?"

"I don't know. Well, I do know, I just don't know how to explain it."

"Try."

"You have no clue what it means to me to hear you say those words. Tristan, I've been in love with you for so long. I just never thought you saw me. I'm the one who no one worries about because I'm me, you know? I just do what I need to do. I didn't know how to make you see me."

"Oh, I saw you." I stepped in closer and pressed a slow kiss to the corner of her mouth. "I've always seen you."

66

Another kiss, but this time, I captured her bottom lip softly between mine. "I only ever want to see you."

A tiny whimper came from her, and then her hands were sinking into my hair and she was tugging me closer, demanding I kiss her without teasing.

"God, do you have any clue what you do to me?"

In a way that only Stella could, she glanced down at my cock, which was demanding to be released from my pants. "Umm, I have a pretty good idea."

With that one sentence, we were ripping at each other's clothes, leaving a pile of garments in the middle of the room.

I trailed kisses along the curve of her neck and tasted the bare traces of her lotion, even that was fucking sexy. Was there anything about this woman that I'd ever not find sexy? "Your skin is so soft," I muttered against her collarbone. "Your skin is like velvet." I trailed the kisses back up until our lips were locked and our tongues were tangled. Pulling her even closer, I lifted her, and she curled around my body, her core resting just above my tip.

"Please tell me that you're on birth control."

"I'm on birth control."

"Tell me that I can cum inside you. I've never been bare, and, God, I want this, I fucking need this with you."

"Tristan, please, just you, nothing else."

A gasp escaped her brightly painted lips as I pressed her back against the wall, my hands found her hips, and the tip of my cock nudged against her opening. For just a second, I paused, overwhelmed by the softness I was desperate to sink into.

Then I was pushing into her.

I couldn't think straight, the wetness, the heat . . . all of it had me fighting back the need to ravage her.

"Harder," she moaned. "Fuck me harder."

I did, and she arched against me so that I could feel my

cock touching places I didn't know I could touch. When she pulled my mouth to hers and demanded I do it again, I grinned.

Her wish was my command.

She seemed lost to the sensations when I spun her away from the wall and laid her back on the bed.

I wanted to feel every pulse, every inch of her, I wanted to rip her climax from her. When I felt the walls of her pussy start to quiver and then tighten, I began to relax the hold that I had on my own restraint.

"That's right, baby, give it to me. Let me hear you."

"Tristan. Please."

"That's my orgasm, give it to me, I want it. I want it now, fucking give it to me, Stella, now." Her body stiffened, her head curved back as her back arched and she shattered and pulsed around me. I followed her over the edge, and the feeling of my cum spilling inside her was unlike anything I'd ever imagined.

God, I wanted this woman forever.

"I love you. I'm so in love with you," I whispered, not knowing if she heard me.

"I love you, too. I always have."

"Marry me." And just like that, it was as if I wanted that more than anything else in the world.

"Whatever you're on, I'll take two. What the ever-loving hell are you saying?"

"You heard me, let's get married. We're in Vegas. Let's get married. Let's not think about it; let's just do it."

"You're serious, aren't you?"

"As a heart attack. What do you say? Up for it, or were you just lying about your feelings for me?"

"I wasn't lying and . . . well . . . okay. Let's get married."

I placed a hungry kiss on her lips. A kiss that said every-thing I'd wanted to say. It was a goodbye to bachelorhood, hello to my wife. It was a holy-shit-she-said-yes kind of kiss. Our tongues tangling around each other's in a dance that was beating to the rhythm of our hearts.

"What are you doing?" she asked as I pulled away and slid from the bed.

"Getting dressed, I want to run downstairs and get a few things in order."

"Like what?"

"Like none of your business." I bent to place a quick kiss on the tip of her nose. "Now, let's get a move on before you change your mind."

She was laughing as I left the room, but I acted all cool as I could until the door clicked shut behind me. Oh my god, I was getting married.

I had nerves of steel, so much so that I could have been a surgeon, but right then, I was shaking so hard I probably wouldn't have been able to tie my own damn shoes. That was why it shocked the shit out of me when I actually managed to make a phone call.

"Hello?"

"Hey, Carter, have a second?"

"Tristan, what's up? Is everything okay?"

"Everything's fine. I just wanted to talk to you about something."

"Sure. Do I need to sit down?" Carter let out a chuckle.

I took a deep breath and, somehow, the words just seemed to pour out. "I know that I should talk to your father, but the truth is, I don't know him and Stella never talks about him. You're who she loves, and as such, I wanted to talk to you."

"Yeah, I need to sit." I could still hear the laughter in Carter's voice.

"I'm in love with Stella. I've been in love with her, and she and I have tried to fight it, but we can't. Every time we decided to give us a try, it seemed like something would happen and she didn't want a relationship between us to take away from someone else's spotlight."

"God, that sounds like her."

"Yeah, but I don't want to give her another chance to get away. I want to marry your sister."

He was silent for so long that I was convinced he was going to tell me to go to hell. Still, I waited.

"Wow," he finally said. "I'm not shocked, but at the same time, I didn't expect it to be this week. Regardless, you're perfect for her, and if she wants to marry you, then that is all that matters to me."

"Thanks. I promise to protect her."

"I know you will."

"Carter?"

"Yes?"

"Please don't tell anyone."

"My lips are sealed. Just do me a favor and don't let anyone know that I knew about it before they did."

I laughed, totally understanding his point. Sophie would give him hell for not spilling the beans. Carter disconnected.

I slid my phone back into my pocket, and my racing heart felt a little lighter. The only thing left to do was organize a wedding.

When I got back to the room, Stella was flipping through the clothes in the closet. "Ugh, I have nothing to wear. I know that we are doing this on the fly, but I'd like something different to wear." She paused for the first time and then turned her attention on me, taking in my wide smile. "What has you so happy?"

"Besides the fact that we are doing something incredibly spontaneous, which may not be such a big deal to you, but for me is out of the norm?"

"Yeah, besides that?"

"How about that, in less than two hours, I will be marrying the love of my life?" Stella pressed her hands against her cheeks as if to physically hold back her blush. "I was thinking—" The knock on the door cut me off, and I felt like a kid on Christmas Day as I went to answer it even though I knew what was behind the door.

After accepting the delivery and tipping the concierge, I turned to show Stella the black formal dress bag and shopping bag.

"I think that I can solve your problem."

She eyed the bags and pulled her bottom lip between her teeth as if unsure about what I'd done.

"What's in those?" she asked, but she didn't move to take the proffered bag.

"It's what you're going to wear." When the personal shopper at Barney's had shown me the dress, I knew it would be breathtaking on her. Stella was gorgeous and this dress was meant for her curves. It wasn't a traditional wedding dress, which was probably what she was thinking, but it was still perfect.

Stella stepped forward and slid the zipper down. She gasped and then reached into the bag. "Lanvin." She traced the white silk before letting her fingers brush over the black beading along the edge of the sleeves. "Tristan, you must have paid a fortune."

Truer words had never been spoken. But to see this look on her face, it made it all worth it. "I can't wait to see it on you."

Gingerly, she traced the deep scoop of the neckline. "It's breathtaking." She had tears welling in the corners of her eyes. "But I don't have shoes."

My answer was to extend the second bag.

Inside, Stella found a pair of silvery white Yves Saint Laurent sling backs and literally went speechless. I mentally noted that shoes were a good way to get her to stop talking and tried not to look like I'd just solved some great world mystery.

"Do you like them?"

"Are you serious? They are beautiful. I can't believe this, I feel very Julia Roberts in *Pretty Woman* at the moment." She snagged the dress bag from me and dashed back to the bedroom, leaving me to collect the bag with my tux in it and follow behind her.

STELLA

"*W*ow, Mr. Christakos, you went all out, didn't you?" I looked from Tristan to the uniformed chauffeur who was holding open the door of a black town car.

"You only get married once."

For him, those words were gospel. I was raised by parents who believed that marriage just meant long-term dating. But Tristan? His parents believed in forever. Me . . . what did I believe in? God, I believed in this man.

Once we were both tucked inside, Tristan opened the center console and pulled out a bottle of chilled champagne and poured it into two flutes. Handing me one, he held his up and stared longingly into my eyes.

"I know that this may seem fast, but it isn't. It's really been a long time coming. If you think about it, we've been learning about each other for the last few years and falling in love with each other just as long. I love your wit, your sass, I love the way you stand up for your friends and are a champion for the underdog. I love how I never have to wonder what you're thinking. Most of all, I love your heart. I promise to treat it as nothing short of precious for as long as you let me." Tristan lifted his glass and clinked it to mine. We sipped then he kissed me, sweeping his tongue against mine in an unhurried dance that promised devotion and loyalty and forever.

We pulled in front of the infamous Chapel of Love and drove under the arched porte cochere.

"You ready?"

I glanced to the closed sunroof and laughed. "I'm so ready. Do you want to do the honors?"

"Absolutely." He pressed a button on the overhead panel, and the sunroof slid open. "After you."

It was a tight fit, but we were both able to stand so we were sticking halfway out of the sunroof. With our fingers laced together, we listened to the minister, who obviously had been a used car saleswoman in a former life, recite some very abbreviated version of a wedding ceremony. "Have you ever noticcced how the wedding ringgg is round? A neverrr-ending circle just like looove." Tristan was grinning, and just like that, we both lost it. The minister didn't seem to take offense or even really notice we were laughing at her ridiculous accent. "You knooow this marriage willlll last, just look at the happinesssss of this younggg couple."

The minister paused and then turned to Tristan. "Are you exchanging rings?"

He reached into his pocket and pulled out an oval-shaped black velvet box. Nestled inside was not one or two rings but three. My bridal set of an engagement and wedding ring and a ring for him. They were breathtaking. I had no clue how he'd had the time to pick them out, but he had.

My ring was absolutely flashy, exactly how I'd like it. Although, it was a simple princess cut it was off set by tons of baguette diamonds encased in the band. "Platinum?"

"Yes," Tristan half-said, half-laughed.

His ring was just as exquisite, a platinum band with three baguette diamonds at an angle. Desperate for him to slide the ring on me, I turned to our former used car saleswoman so she could finish the ceremony.

By the time she pronounced us husband and wife, or as she had said, husbannnd anddd wiiife, my cheeks were hurting from laughing so hard and my heart was bursting with love for this man who I'd harbored a secret love for more than two years.

We didn't parade up and down the strip, honking and shouting. No, instead, Tristan took us back to the hotel and carried me over the threshold.

"Are you hungry, Mrs. Christakos?"

"Yes, hungry for you."

"You're insatiable."

"You know it." I brought my mouth to his and savored the flavors that would be forever marked in my memory.

That night, when we made love, it was different from before. Sure, it was wild and exciting, but there was a passion that could only be explained as love. After, Tristan stayed braced over me, one hand cupping my face as the other brushed the wild blonde hair out of my eyes, and I knew I would never love anyone the way I loved him.

"I think that I could get used to this," he whispered.

"Me, too," I whispered back. Then, being me, I tapped his hip. "Now get off me, I'm hungry."

"Again? You need to give me a few minutes—"

"Ha-ha, no, I meant hungry as in food, real sustenance."

Tristan was grinning as he rolled off. Then, without a care in the world, he marched his naked ass—his gorgeous, well-toned, sun-kissed ass—across the room and grabbed the in-room dining menu.

We ended up ordering pizza and beers, which was not exactly romantic, but it was perfect.

On Saturday, Tristan and I celebrated the fact that we'd been married for one day . . . in bed. Well, that and by ordering room service and watching movies. Come to find out, you could get any movie streamed to your hotel television if you were willing to pay for it. So, we were in hotel robes watching Vacation.

I pointed one finger in the air when it came to Clark's epic tirade about goddamn smiles, whistling zip a dee do dah, and all that other shit and mimicked him word for word. When Clark was done, I was out of breath but something about his temper tantrums always made me feel better, like I had just released the weight of the world from my shoulders.

Tristan held up his hands in surrender. "I believe you."

I leaned back into the curve of his arm and made myself comfortable, not paying attention to what he was doing until I heard a phone ringing.

"Who are you calling?"

"Mana."

"Why?" Tristan tapped my ring. "Don't."

My heart raced, and I was on my knees, trying to get the phone from him. Tristan pressed speakerphone and ignored my spastic outburst. Did he not understand that calling his mother and telling her over the phone that he got married was a terrible, terrible idea?

One ring . . .

Two rings . . .

"Tristan, hey! You having fun?" I think I would have preferred for Tristan's mother to have answered over Kayson. He was as gossipy as a girl, especially with my brother.

"Hey, Kayson, we're having fun. I'm surprised you answered, who all is there?"

"Just about everyone, we had a late dinner. Did you need Mana or Pops?"

"Can you put Mana on?"

"Yep, hold on."

Tristan waited for his mother to come to the phone, and the entire time, I knew that if he told her, she was going to hate me. She didn't get to attend her son's wedding and that would be my fault.

"*Moro mou*, is that you?" Christine's voice rang over the line.

"*Re,* Mana, I have a favor to ask."

Even though I'd been thoroughly ensconced in his family for the last two years, I still got lost with all the Gre-english as I called it, the half-Greek, half-English conversations that his entire family carried on. I knew that *moro mou* meant my son, but that was about it.

"Stella and I have a surprise. When we get back tomorrow, do you care if we come over? We can share it with you all at the same time?"

"Another reason to have my family together? Of course, I don't mind. I'll cook your favorites. Oh, and I know that Stella loves my baklava, so I'll make that as well."

"Thank you, Christine," I said, making sure she could hear me. "That sounds yummy. Will you also make some of your rose candy?"

"Of course, *kouklitsa mou,* I'll make some *loukoumi.*" I glanced at Tristan, raising an eyebrow in silent question. He held up one finger to signal for me to hold on.

"*Agape mou,* Mana, see you tomorrow." He disconnected and then smiled at me. "I have no clue what you are so worried about, my mother loves you."

"What makes you say that?"

"She called you her doll."

~

I TOOK several deep breaths and gripped Tristan's hand tightly as we exited the tram in Orlando International Airport. Lifting my hand, I watched as the sun shining through the glass atrium hit the facets of my diamond. I'd stared at the thing a million times and still found it exquisite. Tristan and I had only been married for exactly one and a half days, so that may wear off . . . in ten or so years.

"Don't look so nervous, Mrs. Christakos." He squeezed my right hand—well, he tried to, but since I had a death grip on him, it wasn't much of a gesture.

"I can't help it. I know the girls are going to kill me for not having them there, and I'm afraid that your mom will be hurt."

"What about your parents?"

"Who cares? My mom doesn't hold a high regard for marriage anyway."

We stepped out of the secure area, and I rummaged in my bag, searching for my phone to call Ariel and let her know that we were on our way to baggage, but Tristan cleared his throat.

"Umm, Stella . . ."

"Hold on, gotta find my phone." I stopped and set my bag down on a bench to search.

"Stella, you may want to look to your right," Tristan warned.

I did and let out a loud laugh. Standing smack dab in the middle of the flow of traffic were Sophie and Ariel, and they were holding signs that read: Welcome home from rehab.

I felt a little verklempt because they just made me so proud. But deciding that there was no way in hell I was going to allow them to one-up me, I gave my bag over to Tristan. Then, in my best impersonation of Phoebe Buffay, I raced toward them, my arms swinging and my legs kicking out side to side as I slammed into them and pulled them into a group hug.

"You three are idiots." Tristan came up behind us and then placed a kiss on top of Ariel and Sophie's heads.

"You two are the best Jedis an evil Yoda could ask for."

Sophia and Ariel exchanged a look, but it was the former who said, "We should be worried, huh?"

"Very."

We cracked up laughing again, but I doubted they knew just how nuts my paybacks could get.

"Why don't you two go get your bags and meet Sophie and me at the arrival loop?"

"Sounds great."

"Why don't you go with them? I can get our bags." Tristan gave me a devilishly wicked smile.

"You sure?"

"I'm sure that there is a lot you all want to catch up on." He winked.

Fuck, he winked. That wasn't suspicious or anything. "I guess so." I took one step, but he stopped me and placed a quick kiss on my lips. In front of our family and friends. In front of people who had no clue we liked each other, let alone got married.

"Let's go. It seems you really do have a lot to fill us in on." Sophie's hand but froze.

Fuck, fuck, fuck. Why did she have to grab my left hand? Jerking my hand up and in front of her face, she let out a scream. An ear-splitting scream. Then, like schoolgirls, Sophie and Ariel were jumping with excitement.

"Holy shit, holy shit, holy shit. Mana is going to be so excited!" Ariel hollered.

"I told you no one would be upset," Tristan whispered in my ear.

"Upset? Are you kidding me? I'm ecstatic." Sophie stared at the ring in awe and then reached for Tristan's hand and examined his ring as well. "Yep, party, definitely a party. Hurry up and go get the luggage. We'll meet you out front."

"We called Mana last night and Tristan asked her to make sure everyone was there for dinner tonight."

I reached for Tristan's laptop case since his hands would be full with our suitcases, Sophie grabbed my backpack, and then we were off.

Sophie grilled me for details the entire way, but when we walked through the tunnel to the parking garage, I turned to Ariel, who was furiously typing out a text.

"Please don't tell anyone, we want to do that."

"Oh, I'm not telling anyone, I'm just making sure everyone is going to be there tonight."

My stomach turned a bit, would everyone be as happy as Sophie and Ariel were?

"YOU KNOW what we're going to say, right?" I asked Tristan as I looked ahead and saw way too many cars to be just family. In fact, there were several motorcycles that I recognized. Motorcycles that belonged to my posse, my tribe. We were a group of women who had bonded over our love for riding motorcycles and had formed an all-ladies club called the Iron Orchids.

"Yes, got it." Tristan stopped walking and pulled me against him. "This feels right. You know that, don't you?"

I nodded.

"Then why are you so worried?"

Taking a deep breath, I let my words fly, "Worried? I'm scared shitless. Me, Stella Lang—oh, wait, Stella Christakos . . . holy shit, I'm Stella Christakos."

Tristan let out a low chuckle. "Did you just now realize that?"

"Yes. I mean, no. I mean, that I realized we were married, but I hadn't said it aloud. I'm Stella fucking Christakos. I like the sound of that."

"So do I."

"But what if your mother is mad and blames me for all this? I mean, what if she thinks that it was my wild ways that tempted you to get married without her even knowing about it?"

"I'll tell her that she's one hundred percent correct, it was all you." Tristan gave me his devilish grin.

I smacked his arms. "Hey, not funny. I'm serious. This is Christine we're talking about. She is like, Mother of the Year, Martha Stewart, and Mary Poppins all rolled up into one person. I don't want her to be disappointed in me."

"She won't be. Mana loves you. She's going to be excited that I'm finally married and closer to giving her grandbabies than worried about not being in Vegas, I promise. The woman has already married off three sons, she has seven brothers, and we have twenty-nine first cousins, of which over half are married, she's had her fill of weddings . . . believe me." Tristan crossed his heart with his index finger. "She'll probably be doing Hail Marys for us taking care of it."

I laughed at him because he had a way of relaxing me.

At exactly seven o'clock, we stepped into Mana and Pops' house. Everyone was out by the pool, obviously waiting for us to arrive. Tristan stood behind me, and I kept my hands tucked into my pockets. "Where's your mom?"

Tristan tilted his head toward the kitchen, where Christine was busy talking to someone on the phone. We headed in there first.

"They're going to find out." Christine was quiet for a few seconds as we walked up behind her.

I turned to Tristan, feeling a bit weary, but he just shrugged it off.

"Okay, let me let you go, they'll be here any moment." She hung up and spun around. "Oh. You're here." Christine reached for Tristan's face and pulled him to her so she could kiss his cheek and then did the same to me. "So, tell me . . . what's the big surprise?"

"Let's go out so we can tell everyone at once."

"Pfft. No, I deserve to know first. After all, I carried you for nine months, and you were the worst—twenty-two hours of labor, let me tell you," Christine said to me.

"Ummm, it was fifteen last time you told the story. I think you said that Kayson was twenty-two," Tristan corrected her.

Christine smacked him upside the head. "I think I would know how long I was in labor, I was there, after all, you impertinent boy." She gave him a wicked smile. "Now, tell me before I have to tell you how I used to walk uphill to school in the snow."

"In Mykonos, Greece?" Tristan raised one eyebrow.

Laughing, Christine brought her hand up again, but Tristan ducked so that she missed smacking him. "Okay, but you have to act surprised when we tell everyone else."

She just rolled her eyes at him. "I'm a very good actress, thank you very much."

Tristan tugged my hand from my pocket and wove our fingers together, it was a sign of solidarity or togetherness, I wasn't sure exactly, but I liked it. Christine let out a scream and then started jumping around kissing Tristan and then kissing me.

"Shhh, Mana, everyone is going to guess if you keep this up, and then there won't be a surprise."

"No, they'll be shocked. Your brothers have a bet on whether you're going to announce that you are officially a couple or that Stella is pregnant. Wait! You aren't pregnant, are you? That would be lovely, as well." Christine reached to pat my belly, but I stepped back.

"No, I'm not pregnant."

"Are you coming out here or not?" We all turned to see Damon standing at the open doors to the lanai. "Sophie and Ariel look like they've swallowed the canary and are dying to tell us but won't. If you don't hurry, they won't be able to keep quiet any longer."

"It's showtime," I whispered.

"Take a deep breath," Christine whispered back. "I've never seen you so nervous."

"I'm happy, I really am, I just don't want anyone be upset with us. Does that make sense?"

"Perfect. Come with me, we won't let anyone ruin this day." Christine wrapped one arm around me, the other around Tristan, and then marched us out to the lanai where our family and friends were gathered.

"About time," Ian hollered.

"What's up?" Damon gave me the once-over.

Christine took a step back and then used her arms to squeeze us together. Suddenly, I felt like a lab rat having everyone staring at me, wondering how I was going to react to some experiment.

Tristan's right hand linked with my left, and he locked eyes with me for a second before turning to the crowd in front of us.

"So we were in Vegas for a genetics conference," Tristan began speaking, but as he did, he brought his left hand up to emphasize his words.

I heard the chuckle first from Ariel and then from Sophie, but a second later, someone gasped. Tristan just continued to talk and wave his hand, completely oblivious to their reactions.

"Freeze!" Kayson hollered just like a cop. "Let me see Stella's left hand."

"Oh, this?" Tristan lifted my hand and showed it to the crowd, and everyone erupted with applause.

I scanned everyone's faces and stopped when my eyes landed on Pops. He was sitting with his arms folded as he watched us. When he caught me looking at him, he winked as if he'd known all along. I turned and looked at Christine, who was still beaming but also had a few tears of happiness in her eyes as she gazed at her husband.

God, this warmed my heart.

Finally, when everyone had quieted and started moving back to the table where food was set out, Pops came up to us.

He placed his hands on my shoulders and stared deep into my eyes. "You are perfect for him. We've always known it." He gave me a light squeeze. "We've always thought of you as a part of our family, but now you know it as well."

I hugged him. "Thanks, George." George lifted one brow. "Does this mean I can call you Pops?"

"I've told you a million times, girl, you've always been allowed to call me Pops."

"Let's eat, I'm starved," Leo hollered as she rubbed her pregnant belly, and just like that, we were back to us and it was like we'd always been a couple. Tristan and I moved to the table and sat together.

"You know what this means, right?" Sophie asked.

"No, what?" I waited for her answer.

"It means that we need to throw a bachelorette party after the fact."

"Oh, great idea. Let's do it this Friday." Ariel clapped her hands together. "I have the perfect idea."

"Whoa. No need for a bachelorette party. Why don't we just do a girls' night out?"

"It will be. Banana's is having a revue, and we were

wanting to go anyway, let's make a night of it." Ariel looked at Kayson for his thoughts.

"Don't look at me, it isn't as if any of you will listen to us anyway." He bent and kissed his wife's nose. She giggled.

"True, but I just wanted to make sure."

"You're good, just no riding motorcycles."

Ariel rolled her eyes, and I laughed. "Really, Kayson? Do you think that I'd fit on a motorcycle right now? Let alone risk being on a bike? Besides, we're going at night. You know that I hate riding at night."

I met Tristan's eyes. "You're okay with it? I mean, this is our honeymoon."

"Go. We will take our honeymoon later, since we both are working this week anyway. Besides, we have to get you moved in." Tristan raised his voice and caught the attention of his brothers. "Hey, who all can help us move Stella's stuff in our house next weekend?"

Our house. Oh my god, Tristan and I had a house. Well, rather, I was moving into Tristan's house and he considered it mine.

TRISTAN

*T*aking a swig of my beer, I leaned back in my chair and smiled. Stella had been nervous, but I knew that they would be happy, mainly because I was happy.

"We're stealing your wife away, okay?" Leo patted my shoulder. I liked how she put the slight inflection at the end of her sentence. It was as if she were asking a question when really her words were purely a courtesy at this point.

"Smile and nod," Ian said from my left.

I smiled and nodded.

"Get used to it. The girls always find time for each other."

"Why not have no phone nights?" I asked, thinking this made total sense.

"You have so much to learn. They're a necessity, it might be important," Kayson mimicked a girl's voice, looking half-amused and half-perturbed by this as he took a seat at the table.

"I'll figure out how to have alone time with Stella."

"Well, you're smarter than I was. Last year, when Leo was having all of her problems, I wanted to be with her every minute just so I knew for my own sanity that she was okay. I mean, someone was framing her, and I couldn't do anything about it, but I wanted to be there just to comfort her. But I couldn't because of work, there is something reassuring just knowing that they have each other."

"They're like a pack," Kayson cut in. "Which is mainly Stella's doing. If anything, we have more to worry about with Stella hanging out with our wives . . ." Kayson's words held no malice, and it made me feel all the better. "I can't explain it, but those women did something, that whole Iron Orchids, motorcycle club was good for them. I know it was for Ariel, and the difference in Leo is unbelievable."

"Sometimes I have to stop and ask myself how many women did I marry?" Carter said, sliding into the seat next to Kayson. "Just wait until you grab the grocery list and have to call your wife so she can decipher the damn thing because there are things not in her handwriting. Leo can't write for shit, but if she's over and drinks all of the lemonade, she'll add it. Stella likes Rice Krispies, so she adds them to the list. All of them do it."

Carter was bitching, but he didn't sound mad. He sounded resolved to his life. "Why don't you tell them to stop?" Kayson, Ian, and Damon all busted out laughing.

"Good luck with that. Learn one thing right now, though. Choose your battles wisely. If you let the little shit go, then when it really matters, she will listen to you," Damon said. "These women are not bad influences on each other—"

Carter let out a loud guffaw and cut off Damon's words.

"No, truthfully, they aren't. They pull some wild-ass pranks, but all in all, none of them would ever cheat or do something illegal. They're great moms. If I made Katy choose between her friends or me, she'd choose me, but she'd be unhappy. I love her too much to ever make her unhappy, so I'll never make her choose."

Kayson held his bottle up and clinked it against Damon's before leaning forward on his elbows. "You told us, you ready to tell work?"

"About us being married?" Kayson nodded. "Hell, yes."

"Are you worried?"

"I've already decided that I'm not going to turn in an expense report, this way, the hospital doesn't feel that we were goofing off on business time."

"Why would they even think that?" Kayson looked perplexed.

"Come on, we go to Vegas not even dating and come back married? Hell, I requested Stella to accompany me. I just don't want them to assume that we manipulated them as a way to pay for our trip."

"Do you really think they will give you trouble?"

"I'm afraid more for her than myself. I don't want to sound cocky, and I know this totally will, but neonatology is in demand; they know that if they give me shit, I can go over to Nemours or Florida Hospital. I love what I do, and I don't care where I do it."

"So, what are the odds that you'll want to drive my car to work sometimes?"

I gave Stella a quick look as I pulled into a spot in the doctor only reserved parking lot. "We can use your car sometimes if you want. I'm just so used to driving mine, I didn't even think about it."

"No. I mean, you. You drive it whether I'm with you or not?"

"You mean like if my car's broken down?" I was totally lost.

Stella threw her hands into the air, totally exasperated

with me. "I guess that I'm going to have to spell it out for you. Have you ever seen where we have to park? We, as in nurses and normal hospital staff?"

I shook my head.

"Exactly. I want to know what the odds are of you getting one of those nifty little stickers for my car so I can park closer than fucking handicap."

"Fine, I know what to get you for Christmas." I leaned over and pulled her face to mine. "Are you ready, Mrs. Christakos?"

"Ready for twenty questions? Ready to have everyone assume that I'm pregnant and gossip about it? Sure . . . let's go."

Our first stop was Mrs. Cameron's office. I felt it was the wisest move to explain first than to try and explain later after she found out through the gossip mill. Because shit like a doctor and nurse getting married would spread. Plus, Stella needed to change her address on file with the hospital.

I rubbed my palms along the tops of my thighs like a nervous schoolboy sitting in front of the principal.

"It's weird," Mrs. Cameron said, her voice almost a whisper.

"What is?"

"I'm shocked but, at the same time, I'm not."

"You're shocked by him and totally not by me, right?" Stella asked, totally at ease.

"I don't think that's it. I think that I'm not shocked that the two of you got married. I'm shocked that it happened this past week though."

"Don't worry, I already decided not to turn in an expense report. Even though we decided this after the conference was totally over, I didn't want any conflicts of interest."

"Dr. Christakos, you're the last person I'd worry about

trying to take advantage of the hospital. Turn your form in for the daily per diems."

"Thank you." I stood, said my goodbye to Louise Cameron, and then escorted Stella out.

Stella wiped her hand across her brow. "Wow, that went a lot smoother than I thought it would."

"You were nervous?"

"Well, I wasn't exactly sure how it was all going to turn out. Hey, I better get over to the ER."

"Send me a text when you're headed to lunch, if I can run down and meet you, I will. If not, maybe you could come have lunch with me in my office?"

"I think I might be able to manage that."

I gave her a quick peck before we split and went our separate ways.

"Hey." I stopped and turned, taking in the twinkle in her eyes. "Don't get used to telling me what to do. It's only because I haven't gotten tired of you yet."

"What have I gotten myself into?"

"Don't say I didn't warn you."

I ran one hand through my hair as I tried to catch up to where Stella's mind was going. "You didn't warn me about what?"

"Nooo, remember, my wedding vows to you were, 'You can't say I didn't warn you.'"

I laughed. "Yeah, you warned me, but I was willing to take a chance. I decided that I'd keep your mouth occupied doing other things." I wrapped one arm around her.

"Don't. Anyone can see us." Stella pushed my arm away.

"I don't care."

"I do. You won't get shit, I'll get shit, and then I'll have to lose said shit on someone, and I really hate looking like a bitch."

"Just looking?"

"Bite me."

I chuckled. "See you at lunch." I headed to neonatology and tried to figure out how long it would take for someone to notice the platinum band on my third finger . . . a lot faster than I'd imagined.

I grabbed the stack of files out of the bin marked with my name and rounded the corner when I overheard one of the nurses ask, "Did he have a wedding band on?"

"No. He isn't seeing anyone."

"I swear I think he's wearing a wedding band."

"Then, why would he be here today? Wouldn't he be away on his honeymoon?" The second, older nurse tried to reason.

"He was gone all last week," another nurse reminded them.

"Someone needs to go talk to him and get a better look."

"Really? None of us work with him, it would be kind of strange."

I smiled and kept walking. I could see Stella's point—this was going to cause a lot of gossip, and for the first time, I was okay with it.

The morning dragged by, and I found myself spending most of my time in my office catching up on everything I'd missed last week. At noon, my phone buzzed, and I grinned when I saw who was texting me.

STELLA: Going to lunch.

Stella: I'll just grab you something.

Stella: On my way now.

SHIT.

I hated when messages got caught up and then all came

through at once. Sliding my phone back onto my belt, I pushed away from my desk and headed for the elevator, not sure how long ago she'd actually sent those messages. The least I could do was help her carry the food, but when I hit the hallway, I pulled to a stop.

"I didn't think you worked on this floor anymore."

"I don't, I'm meeting someone for lunch." To most people, Stella's words probably sounded like sugar, but I recognized the acid slowly building.

"Oh, you must be lost, the cafeteria is—"

"Don't play a game of wits with me, you'll find out just how unarmed you really are. I know where the cafeteria is. I'm meeting Tristan, he's expecting me."

"He didn't tell us. We'll need to buzz him."

"You're a nurse, just like I'm a nurse, and we both know there's no buzzing. Stop with the cattiness."

Okay, okay, this was when any sane man would walk out and stop the situation, but I never claimed to be sane.

"Miss Lang, I'm sorry but—"

"Okay, Bertha or whatever your name is, I get that we didn't work together long, so you don't really know me, but I'm going to let you in on something, my name isn't Miss Lang."

"It isn't? Aren't you Stella Lang?"

"I was. Now, I'm Stella Christakos, and if you don't mind, I'm taking lunch to my husband, who is expecting me." Stella took two steps, stopped, and said, "Close your mouth there, Bertha." She walked around the corner, almost running right into me as she did.

I reached out and caught the food before she dropped it and placed one arm around her.

"You ass, how long were you standing there?"

"Not long, I promise. Let's go eat, Mrs. Christakos."

"Fuck you, fuck you big time," Stella seethed, more toward the nurse she'd just put in her place than at me.

This mood was no good, though, so I bent closer to her and whispered, "So what's really for lunch? I see a lot that I could eat."

"*Y*ou know how weird this is, right?" Piper held Stella's hand and examined the ring. "It's been two years since we formed Iron Orchids, and the four of you are married, but I'm still no closer to finding a man."

"Umm, me neither," Everly cut in.

"Or me," Vivian added.

I was glad to see that Vivian was finally talking about men again. It had been almost three years since she lost her husband while in the line of duty, and for a while, I was seriously worried about her snapping out of her depression.

"Maybe you've already met him at work and you just need to be whisked away."

"Great, that leaves my choices as Carter and Kayson, who are already taken, or one of the other deputies who do nothing to turn me on." Piper puffed out some air to blow her hair out of her eyes.

"You never know, maybe you'll be one of those prison women who falls for an inmate," I offered.

"I think not." She punched me in the arm.

"I'm not sure if I'll ever find someone again, but if I don't, at least I can say that I knew what it was like to be loved completely." Vivian's words were soft.

It was the old question of whether it was better to have loved and lost or never to have loved at all. And the truth was, I had no fucking clue.

"Well, I'm not settling for one of the paramedics or firemen. I have to bunk with them for twenty-four hours at a time. I know their habits, and none of them are worth committing to for a lifetime. I think that I might convert to Catholicism and become a nun rather than tie myself down to their slob asses."

We all laughed as we moved forward in the line. Although Banana's was a well-known drag-show restaurant and one that we'd never been able to convince any of the guys to come to, the number of men that I saw in line never ceased to amaze me. Some looked happy, some looked none too pleased, and some looked . . . well, as if they'd been drugged or blackmailed into coming. It had become a game with us to try to figure out what each guy's story was and why he was here.

"Look at that guy, the one in the Old Navy shirt." I gave a chin nod in his direction.

Piper turned to see who I'd been talking about. "Crossed arms, legs spread wide. Oh, he's a tough one, all right. He wants everyone to know that he came here under duress."

"He's saying he has a stick up his ass and he'd like someone to pull it out," I quipped.

"How 'bout him?" Ariel pointed to a man in a red shirt and khaki shorts.

"Besides the fact that he looks as if he just got off from a shift at Target? He is here for the entertainment. Look at him —he's radiating excitement. I love it." I twisted my head around and continued to take in people as we moved closer to the front doors.

We finally made our way inside and the place was hopping. Banana's was usually set up to look like a fifties-style diner with waitresses wearing nametags that said Alice. The performers usually wore tabernacle choir robes and bouffant hairdos as they sang old church hymns. But for tonight the place had a facelift. The waiters—or rather, waitresses—were dressed as Ethel Merman a la her later years with chiffon robes over silk jumpsuits, tiny tiaras, and huge gemstone earrings. They walked around singing, *There's No Business Like Show Business* or the other Ethel classic, *Everything's Coming Up Roses- For me*.

"Ladies, Ringo reserved a table for you upfront. You should see your name." The hostess, who was the spitting image of Diana Ross, pointed to the front corner.

We wound our way through the room, the place was crowded and they had replaced the large dining tables for smaller cocktail tables.

"I see Christakos on that table over there." Ariel pulled my hand as we moved around a group of women. Once we were seated, Ariel opened her bag and pulled out a tiara and handed it to me.

"I'm not wearing this."

"The fuck you say? You embarrassed the hell out of me at my bachelorette party. We were busted by the cops. The least you can do is wear a damn tiara."

"Fine." I shoved it on my head. Ariel handed tiaras out to everyone else along with clackers, whistles, beads, and boas. "Holy shit, what else do you have in there?" I reached for her bag.

"Nothing. I promise. They're selling alcohol so there was no need to smuggle any in, and with two of us pregnant and one nursing, you know that you are guaranteed designated drivers."

"Excuse me."

We all stopped talking to turn and look at the gorgeous brunette at the table next to us. She was sitting with four other ladies and they all appeared a bit uptight for my taste.

"I saw the name Christakos on the table and figured that it couldn't be that common of a name. Who is a Christakos?"

Ariel, Leo, Katy, me, and even Sophie raised our hands. Sophie was technically a Lang since she was married to my brother, but not a single one of us cared.

The woman let out a laugh. "Okay. So, it's true what they say about Greeks, you're all related?" We nodded, and the woman asked, "Is one of you related to Ian Christakos?"

Leo spoke up. "We all are, but I'm his wife."

"It's so nice to meet you. How are you feeling?"

I was taken aback by the woman's instant kinship with Leo. Obviously, whoever she was she knew Ian and he talked about Leo all the time.

"I'm fine," Leo said, more than a little apprehensive.

I laughed when one of the woman's friends elbowed her and said something.

"Oh my god, I didn't even introduce myself. I'm Lara Bradford, I've worked with Ian on a number of projects and he's told me a lot about you. Although, he's refused to let us meet. He says that I'm too much like someone named Stella."

I raised my hand. "That would be me."

"Oh, are you someone who can't be put on speakerphone because you'll say what everyone else is thinking?" Leo asked. Lara's friends laughed and gave a resounding yes. "Then you and Stella are most definitely alike."

"You're an engineer?" I asked because I could never imagine myself as an engineer.

"No, I'm a Major in the US Army. I work over at PEOStri. This is Kennedy, Pilar, Brynn, and Georgia."

"Are all of you in the Army, too?"

"Yes," the one I think that she said was Pilar replied.

Leo introduced all of us, and before we knew it, we were sliding back and pushing our tables together.

"By the way, Leo, I wanted to talk with you. We all ride."

"What?" I interrupted. "We have a gang, you should join us."

"It isn't a gang," Ariel said, exasperated.

"Whatever." I waved my hand in the air totally dismissing her.

"Absolutely. I wanted to talk with Leo about ordering some parts for my bike anyway. We'll exchange numbers . . ." But Lara's words were cut off by the darkening of the house lights and the rolling of a drumbeat.

"Ladies and . . . well . . . lady wannabees, are you ready for tonight?" the emcee said, but I missed the rest of his introduction because all I could hear was some dumbass man.

"This is fucking stupid, I can't believe this is what you brought me to."

"Shhh. Please."

Trying to ignore the asshat, I turned my focus back to the show. "In the center of your tables, you will each see several flashcards with numbers one through ten. After each act we will ask you to give us your score. That's right, you are the judges this evening."

The room erupted in shouts, everyone obviously happy with the thought of having such an active part in tonight's show.

"You'll have to work together as a team to come up with your score, and we'll have tallywackers—" The emcee paused and waited for everyone's laughter to die down, which, of course, gave the guy plenty of time to slip in another snide remark.

"Does he think he's funny?"

I felt nails sink into my flesh, and I turned to see Ariel shaking her head. "Stay calm, this isn't our fight."

"Then he needs to shut the fuck up and not bring everyone around him into it."

The emcee continued, "I'm sorry, I meant to say counters who will tally up your numbers after each performance. So, make sure to hold your numbers high and keep them up until we tell you otherwise. Let's give it a run through. Go ahead, appoint a scorekeeper and hold up a card."

"We have two sets, I guess since we're two tables pushed together." Ariel grabbed the two sets since they were in front of her and slid one to Lara, who turned to me.

"Stella, you take one since it's your night tonight." She leaned over and whispered, "And maybe it will keep you focused on something other than killing this man at the table next to us."

Deciding that she was right and that I wasn't going to let him ruin my fun, I snatched it from her. "Fuck, yeah. I'll make those bitches cry. Simon Cowell has nothing on me." Vivian took the other set to be the yin to my yang. I found the number ten and held it up along with everyone else.

"Perfect. You all passed the first test. Now, let's get the show started."

We all applauded, and while we waited, a server came by and took our orders. There were only drinks and finger foods tonight, but that was great by me.

"I'd like a steak."

"Sir, we are only serving appetizers tonight. We don't have a full kitchen staff," the server explained to asshat.

"This is a restaurant, isn't it?"

"Yes, but tonight is a special night, and it is after normal dinner hours. We have appetizers."

"You also have paying guests."

"Ughhh." I turned my focus on him and stared.

"Mind your own fucking business," he hollered to me.

"It's kind of hard when you're being an obnoxious asshat and interrupting the fucking show."

"Bitch."

Oh, no, he didn't. I wasn't sure whether I was the first one to stand or the last, but all the Iron Orchids, as well as Lara and her military friends were on our feet. "Listen, mother-fucker, call me a bitch again and we'll be calling you an ambulance." I crossed my arms and was in the stare match of all stare matches.

"Okay, let's sit, we've made it bad enough," Ariel said, trying to defuse the situation.

"No, I think that I can still make it worse." When I turned back to the table behind us, I looked straight at the woman seated to asshat's left. "Sweetheart, I feel sorry for you."

"Tell me about it," she mumbled.

"Obviously, the only dick you're getting is from his attitude."

Lara wrapped her arm around my shoulders. "Yep, totally understand what Ian meant now. I think this asshole needs to be escorted out."

"On it." Piper stood and walked around the table and over to the man.

I watched as Brynn, who'd been sitting quietly toward the back corner of Lara's table, stood and moved.

"What's she doing?" I asked Lara.

"She's military police. I'm assuming that she is just watching in case Piper needs assistance. He's a big guy, after all."

"She sent a text to someone before she headed over to him. So there should be an officer on his way," Leo said.

We watched as Piper flashed her badge, and the guy pushed out his chest, balled up his fist, and then thought better of it. Piper kept her words low, but we were close enough to still hear her ask him to leave quietly. Naturally, he declined.

"Come on, Sarah, let's go." He stood and reached for his date, but she stayed seated. "I said let's go."

"No. I came to see this show. You were the asshole, not me, why should I leave?"

"I'm not waiting for you, you'll have to fucking walk to your house."

"We'll take her," I offered and then gave the asshole a wide smile.

He stormed out, and Piper followed him. Once he was out, everyone clapped.

"Now, wasn't that special?" the emcee said.

"Sarah, want to join us?" We scooted our chairs and made room for her. She grabbed her drink and moved over.

"We'll begin in five minutes," the emcee warned.

Piper rejoined us.

"I'm so sorry about Eddie. We've only gone out a few times, but it's my birthday so I said I wanted to see this show."

"No apologies. Happy Birthday, we will make it fun."

Sarah was staring at Everly. "Don't I know you?"

"I don't think so." Everly looked puzzled

"Are you with the Orange County Fire Department?"

"Yes, how'd you know?"

"I just transferred over to this area. You're at house fifty-two, right?"

Everly nodded.

"I'm at fifty-seven, we were both at that warehouse fire on Oakridge. I'm Hazmat."

Their conversation was cut off by the lights going dark once again. Our first entertainer lip-synced, but was a dead ringer for Dolly Parton. I deducted points for lip-syncing, which probably wasn't very fair, but Ringo set that bar way too high for me to ignore it.

Leaning over to Lara's table. "Do you all know Ringo? He's generally the headliner here." When they said no, I grinned. "Oh, just you wait, he has the voice of an angel. He sings like Whitney, no joke."

"He is so fuckin' funny," Ariel added in.

"My daughter adores him," Katy told them.

"This is our first time here," Kennedy told us.

Entertainer after entertainer came across the stage, some actually sang, but I held on to my number ten. I wasn't giving that out to anyone but Ringo.

We were on our third round of drinks when the lights were dimmed again and the strum from a ukulele echoed all around. A single spotlight landed on someone sitting in what looked like a windowsill.

We were on our feet as Ringo appeared, wearing a brown wig and a bandana tied around his head. He hung out of the makeshift window, looking like Audrey Hepburn—well, Audrey Hepburn with a much warmer skin tone. He strummed the ukulele and sang "Moon River." Not lip-synced, but motherfucking sang.

Before the announcer could even ask, I had my ten up and was jumping and shouting. Ringo looked out at us and winked.

TRISTAN

*I*nching the covers down Stella's back, I lifted the hem of her shirt or rather my T-shirt since that was what she had commandeered to sleep in and began kissing along her spine.

"Go away, my husband will be back any moment."

"Excuse me." I bent and bit her left butt cheek.

"Oww. Don't do that, Liam, if you leave a mark, he'll see."

"Liam? Who the fuck is Liam?" I could totally tell that she was joking.

She flopped over onto her back and was wearing a smirk. "Tristan, hi. When did you get back?"

I crooked one eyebrow. "Care to tell me about this Liam fellow?"

I laughed at Stella's mock horror. "Liam. Ummm, whatever are you talking about?"

Straddling her, I slid my fingers up and under her shirt and began tickling her. She kicked her long legs out, trying to buck me off. "Okay, okay. Liam Hemsworth, Liam Hemsworth. Well, truthfully, I'd call for Chris, but Liam sounds so much sexier to call out in passion, doesn't it?"

"I wouldn't know." I cracked up laughing at the way her brain worked. "Where was I now?" Lowering my head back down, I returned to biting and nipping. I had no intention of getting out of bed anytime soon. We'd been married exactly one week, and I wanted to enjoy a few hours before we had to face the morning. Soon enough, we'd have to become responsible adults who met my family at her townhouse to help pack up her stuff.

I took my time cherishing my wife's body, showing her exactly how much I appreciated the fact that she'd said yes. So much so, I made her say—or rather, shout—yes a few times before we finally accepted that our time this morning was over.

"You get ready, I'll get our coffee." I wasn't sure why I said anything since this had become our routine, one in which I thoroughly enjoyed, and it was a given that since she took longer she'd go first in the bathroom.

While the coffee percolated, I pulled down two mugs from the cabinet before adding cream and sugar in hers and just sugar in mine. Then taking them back to the bathroom where we both got ready side by side. A feeling washed over me, a sort of contentment.

This, being here with her, felt *right*.

Less than thirty minutes later, we pulled into Stella's driveway.

"Wow, the realtor wastes no time, does she?" There was a large for sale sign in front of Stella's house.

Opening the back of my Lexus, I pulled out the boxes I'd picked up earlier in the week and grabbed the bag of markers and packing tape. Of course, Stella was no help, her hands were full and so was her mouth. We'd stopped to pick up a few dozen fresh Krispy Kreme donuts and Stella was more occupied with eating them than carrying in boxes.

When we got inside, Stella put on a pot of coffee, and I

started assembling boxes. Any minute the cavalry would be here and we'd get this place loaded in no time.

"Are you okay with this move?" This had to be a lot on her, and even though she hadn't said anything, I still wanted to make sure. She was the one giving up so much for me. She gave up her last name for mine. She was giving up her home for mine . . . granted mine was much larger and an actual home with property, not a small townhome, but still, this was hers. She was even giving up some of her stuff since we didn't need duplicates. Sure, she'd decided that my furniture and appliances were newer—or, as she'd put it, *"Cost a whole fuck of a lot more,"* so those were the ones we were keeping, but I still felt as if the give and take wasn't balanced.

"Any happier there'd have to be two of me." Stella gave me a kiss.

"Break it up, none of that shit," Carter ordered as he came in rolling a handcart.

"Hell's bells, Stella, I never realized how small this place was until we all piled in here," Ariel announced as she moved to the couch and sat.

"Maybe that's because you're ready to pop any day."

Ariel froze with a donut halfway to her mouth, her eyes filling with tears as she stared at Stella. "Are you saying that the place seems small because I'm huge?"

"Oh my god! No! I was joking. You are one of the most beautiful pregnant women I have ever met." Stella threw herself at her friend and was hugging her as she begged her forgiveness. If she hadn't been hugging her, she would have seen Ariel wink at us.

"Whatever. You're forgiven." Ariel pulled back, took a giant bite of her donut, and then flipped her notebook open on her lap. "Why don't Stella and I start in her bedroom and bathroom since most of that stuff will be boxed and taken to the house? How about the living room? Is anything in here or are your barstools going to y'all's house?" Ariel looked at me, and I looked at Stella.

"No. All of it is going into storage until we can decide who needs what or where it's going. I figured we'd probably put my televisions into the guest rooms, but not right now."

"Sophie, why don't you and Katy start boxing up her kitchen stuff? Perishable items we'll send home with them and I'm assuming that everything else goes to storage?"

Ariel looked at Stella for confirmation.

"Except my wine glasses, those are coming with me."

"Of course they are." I chuckled.

"Leo, if you can start boxing up the few things in the guest bathroom that would be great." Leo nodded, and Ariel shoved her notepad back into her purse. "You heard her, boys, y'all can start in here." Kayson reached out and helped hoist his wife up. Stella and Ariel each took a few boxes and headed back to her bedroom, but Sophie sidled up next to me.

"How do you like being married?"

"I've never been happier."

"I can tell. I've never seen you smile so much. You two really are perfect together, but then again, I've always thought that you would be."

"Did Carter tell you that I called him?"

"Yes and thank you, that really meant a lot to him. He's always worried about her but I think that he knows you are what is right for her. The two of you just work."

"Stella was so worried that people would blame her, thinking that this was all her idea, that I couldn't be spontaneous."

"Are you kidding me? You're more like her than you think. Of all the boys, you were always the trickster. I knew that you were going to be blunt with me. Damon was going to do whatever he could to not hurt my feelings, Ian was just going to listen to me and seldom say anything back unless he researched it, Kayson and I were so close that he was usually in whatever trouble with me, but you . . . you were different. I always knew that I could come to you and that you'd say it like it was. Now I'm just wondering how long it's going to take before you have the mouth of a trucker."

"I read something about how people who cuss more are the most honest people. For some reason, the filter that forces you to behave a certain way is the same filter that makes you be someone that you aren't. It is literally a fakeness filter. People who cuss more don't have it and end up being loyal to a fault."

"Wow, that describes Stella to a T. It also describes you. Do you cuss a lot more than I hear?" Sophie gave me a side-eye.

I chuckled. "I cuss a lot in my head, all the fucking time. But since I'm around babies and parents, I try to rein it in."

"You two going to stand around and shoot the shit or are you actually going to help?" Damon asked as he tossed me a pair of gloves.

"Fine." I caught them and then shoved my hands into them. "Thanks, Soph, love ya."

"I know. I'm just lovable that way."

I moved into the living room and grabbed one end of the coffee table while Damon had ahold of the other, I got stuck walking backward. We carried it outside and loaded it into his truck.

Then we headed in, and with Ian's help, we grabbed her sofa and added that to a truck as well. When the living room was empty, Damon and Carter moved into the kitchen to move the table and chairs before starting on the boxes the girls had packed.

I headed back to the bedroom to see what my wife was up to. God, I loved saying that. "How you doing in here?"

"We're good," Stella said from her perch on the trunk at the base of her bed. "I've loaded everything that I want to keep with me into here. Do we have room at your house for the trunk?"

"At our house?" I corrected her. She blushed. Holy hell, Stella blushed.

"Fine, our house." She put emphasis on the word *our*.

"Yes."

"We don't have to put it in the bedroom, we can store it anywhere."

"Or we can put it at the foot of our bed," I said as I stepped closer to her. "If that's where you like it."

She nodded.

I leaned down and placed a quick kiss on her lips. "Is making you happy always gonna be this easy?"

Stella gave me a shy grin then let out an evil cackle.

"I take that as a no."

Standing, she patted my chest. "Big no, hard no, huge no."

DISCOVERING other ways to make Stella happy was purely happenstance.

I discovered that some women were like barracudas and went after shiny things in the water, but there were others who went after shiny things at work. Like men wearing shiny wedding bands.

I wasn't sure why it happened, but as soon as word spread that a man was off the market, barracuda-like women seemed to come out of the cracks and crevices to proclaim their interest. I figured it was that tiny object around that fourth finger. I really needed to ask my brother, Ian, about this, I was sure he had some graph he'd drawn up on the subject.

And Stella . . . well, she was happy being a grenade, going off on anything that got too close to her possessions. And that ring she placed on my finger was definitely hers.

"Dr. Christakos, how's married life treating you?"

I smiled at one of the nurses approaching, she was totally opposite of Stella. Dark where Stella was light, short where Stella was tall. "Great, thanks for asking, Teena."

"I can't believe you did it, I always thought that you would be a bachelor forever."

"Nope. I've always been a family man, I was just waiting for the right woman."

"I hear that she's a nurse here in the hospital, I look forward to meeting her. But you know many couples stray, it's hard to work together and play together."

I shifted, totally uncomfortable by this conversation, and glanced toward the bank of elevators in time to see the doors of the one on the left open to reveal Stella standing inside.

"Yes, she's a nurse, and nope, Stella and I have been working together and as you put it playing together for years. She's very close to my family."

"Well, if you ever change your mind, I know several people who wouldn't mind helping you stray, myself included."

"Stray? Are you getting a stray dog?" Stella grinned as she sidled up in front of me and wrapped her arms around my waist. "But, honey, you know how much I hate mangy mutts. They always have fleas." Then she turned toward Teena. "I even hear that some have twat fleas. Oh, god, I'm so rude, let me introduce myself, I'm his playground—I mean, his wife. And you are?"

Teena turned and walked off.

"I'm sorry, I didn't get Fido's name."

"Okay, Stel, you've made your point."

"Fluffy, come here, fluffy." Stella patted her thigh as if calling a dog.

I shook my head, knowing that there was no use trying to stop her.

"Oh, this is going to be so much fun. I'm going to start bringing in chew toys for her."

"You do realize that this is why people are scared of you, don't you?"

"Yep."

I used to joke about the type of man it would take to handle her, and I only just realized that the man I'd been joking about had been me all along.

TRISTAN

"*Y*ou coming to bed?"

"Not right now."

"What's on your mind?"

I turned down the volume on the television. "Bad day, we lost Grace, I really thought she was going to pull through. God, her parents were devastated. Her mother, you should have heard her, it was so sad. All she kept asking was, if there was anything else that she could have done while she was pregnant? She's blaming herself."

"And you're blaming yourself." Stella curled up on the couch and rested her feet in my lap. "I know you. I know that you did everything possible to save that little girl. But you and I both know that, no matter how advanced the medical treatment, sometimes, it isn't enough."

I nodded because she was right. It didn't make it any easier, but she was right.

"Want some alone time?"

"No. I like having you here. Believe it or not, you're help-ing." We sat in silence for a few more minutes, and I turned the volume on the movie back up. I hadn't really been paying attention to what was playing before Stella came out so I was trying to catch up. "Have you seen this before?"

"Yeah, it's sort of a girl classic."

"Why is everyone making fun of her?"

"Julia Roberts is the runaway bride, she has been engaged several times, and each time she gets to the aisle, she can't go through with the wedding. Something makes her realize that it isn't right, so she bolts, which is why her dad calls her Bolt."

"And him, what's Richard Gere doing?"

"He was going to do an article on her and expose her as sort of a ball-breaker, but he's falling in love with her."

I shook my head at the god-awful romantic attempts. "It's totally her fault. She doesn't even know what she wants, so she's giving mixed signals. Hell, if she'd settled with any of them, she would just end up resenting them. Only, it wouldn't be from anything they did. It would be because she was lying to herself the whole time."

"True, but sometimes it's hard to know exactly what you want when you're swept up in the moment." Something about Stella's words niggled at the back of my head. The movie kept playing, and I weighed the pros and cons of asking the question I wanted to ask.

Curiosity got the better of me, and when the credits started to roll, I shifted to look at her. "If you could go back and change anything about our wedding, would you?"

Stella pulled her thumb up to her lips and started chewing on her nail. "Probably just our friends and family, I hate that they weren't there. Don't get me wrong, I totally love the whole spontaneous part of it, that is so me. I just wish they'd been there to at least laugh with us at the used car salesman minister."

"Some day, we will renew our vows, and when we do, I promise they will be there."

FOR THE NEXT THREE WEEKS, Stella and I had fell into place. There was no better way to say it than that. Incredible as it sounded, it was hard to imagine my house without her. I totally understood why Pops and my brothers loved getting home from work and why they were no longer workaholics. When Stella wasn't at work, I didn't want to be at work either, which was why I was cutting out a half hour early.

"I'm out of here," I said to Dr. Ahmendel, who was the on-call doctor tonight. "I changed the medication schedule for the McIntyre baby and left notes in the file for you."

"Thanks, Tristan. Have a good night."

Standing in front of the elevator, I groaned when a particular reflection came up behind me.

"I have to thank you, Tristan."

"Why is that?" I asked said reflection, not really wanting to make small talk with the guy behind me. For some reason, he thought that we were friends, but in reality, I despised him and everything about him. I pressed the down button and then pressed it again. It was one of those things you did to look busy and avoid those around you. Unfortunately, he didn't get the hint.

"It didn't take long for word to get around that you were off the market. You just widened my dating pool to all the nurses who were secretly holding out for you."

I turned and stared at him. "Well, I guess that's good news for you. I'm not sure that dating subordinates is a good idea, though."

"Says the man who married a nurse."

"Yeah, well, Stella and I have known each other outside of work for years." I didn't tell him that she and I never dated or that we got married on a whim. This guy wasn't getting that type of ammo from me.

The elevator doors opened, and we stepped in. I seriously hoped he'd shut up since there were two other people near us.

He just lowered his voice and held up his hand in mock horror. "Fine, then I just won't date my subordinates. Thanks for the advice." He chuckled. He fucking chuckled at what he thought was a funny joke to hint around that he only used the nurses for sex. "You're a stronger man than I am, committing to one person. But, hey, like they say, just because you've ordered dinner doesn't mean you can't still look at the menu, does it?"

The last thing any of us needed was for him to say something like that around Stella because I wasn't sure that I had enough bail money to get someone out who was charged with murder. "The man who said that probably didn't have a woman like Stella waiting for him at home. Speaking of which . . ."

I pulled my phone out and scrolled to her number, which she's relabeled as Ball and Chain, and headed to my car.

"Talk to me, Goose," she answered.

I laughed. "I'm on my way home, Maverick, need me to pick up anything?"

"Nope, I'm good. See you soon."

I disconnected and felt an ache in my face, my cheeks hurt. Ever since Stella moved into my life, I smiled a lot more. My wife meant everything to me.

God, *my wife*. I loved saying that, would I ever get tired of it? I maneuvered my Lexus RC F around some obviously lost tourist who didn't have enough sense to pull over while they looked at maps on their phones. Cutting through back streets, I pulled into my driveway ten minutes later than I would have if I'd stayed on I-4.

When I opened the door, my eyes landed on Stella, who was bent over the stove, her gorgeous ass was propped in the air, begging to be grabbed, and well . . . I was just the man to grab it. Of course, I waited until she was in no danger of burning herself, I wasn't a complete jerk.

In the fourteen years between starting college and becoming a full-fledge neonatologist, there hadn't been a lot of time for girls. So, this, having her in my home, sleeping next to her, waking up next to her . . . it was totally new for me, and I loved it.

I stroked my hands along her curvaceous hips before pulling her back against me, knowing full well that she could feel my growing erection.

"Why, Mr. Christakos, whatever do you think you are doing?"

"I'm examining Mrs. Christakos's ass. I think that I need you to strip so I can get a better look."

"Is that doctor's orders?"

"Hell, fucking, yes it is."

She stood straight, and with one foot, I kicked the oven door closed.

"In a hurry?" She laughed.

"In a hurry to be inside you."

"Good, the lasagna has to cook for an hour." Stella set the timer but, of course, wiggled her ass as she did.

I slid my hands around to the front of her jeans and unsnapped them before hooking my fingers through the belt loops and easing them down her legs. I knelt while I helped her out of the skintight denim and then slowly made my way back up by placing kisses along the back of her calves. Kiss... her knees. Kiss...her thighs. And, bite...one perfectly round ass cheek.

Once again standing, I made quick work of her shirt and bra, I tossed them to the floor where they formed a pile along with her jeans. All that was left were her panties, if one could call them that, they were more like a piece of string and lace, bright red lace.

"Hey, no fair," Stella whined.

"Are you complaining?" I slid one hand down her side and then around to her front, slipping my fingers under the elastic of her panties and between the folds of her pussy. "Are you sure that you're not complaining?"

She just shook her head and shuttered as I teased her clit. Then, ever so slowly, I walked her toward the edge of the kitchen bar. "Place both hands on the bar and spread your legs. Don't let go unless I tell you to let go, do you hear me?"

She nodded. "Uh-huh."

"I like you like this."

"Like what?" she panted.

"Docile. You're so strong." I licked around her shoulder blade. "So in control." I grazed my teeth over the area where my tongue had just been. "But the fact that you let me be in-charge and your utter trust in me is . . ." I dragged my face across her velvety smooth skin and loved the way she arched. "It's intoxicating. You're mine, finally."

I'd never imagined myself being so dominant but with Stella everything was always a power struggle. She was larger than life, always taking the lead, and I never wanted to break that spirit but in sex, I wanted to show her that she could let loose.

"Do you trust me?" I asked.

"Yes. Now just fuck me, stop with the games, I need you."

I laughed, and a small part of me felt guilty for prolonging her tantalizing agony, but I knew that deep down she loved it just as I did.

"Why in such a hurry?" I ran my fingers lightly down her arms until tiny goose bumps prickled. "We have the rest of our lives."

"Yeah, well, I'd like more than one orgasm in that lifetime so hurry the fuck up."

My fingers teased along the edge of her panties as I peppered slow, open-mouthed kisses down her spine. The lower my kisses went, the lower her panties went, and eventually they were hooked around her ankles and I was kneeling behind her.

I smiled at the feel of Stella's legs tensing in anticipation, wrapping my hands around her legs, she relaxed. When my tongue darted out and along her clit, she became pliable. "That's right, enjoy. Let me take care of you." My words vibrated against her core and she shivered. "You're so beautiful." With one long stroke of my tongue, I glided through her folds and tasted her desire for me. There was nothing that could build a man's self esteem more than seeing what he did to a woman...his woman.

Licking my lips and savoring every drop of her sweet dew, I slid my hands ever so slowly up her firm thighs until her words had become inaudible and all I heard were moans of desire and cries of pleasure.

"Tristan, yes. God, that feels so good."

I wanted her lips, I wanted to kiss her and let her taste herself on me. A mingling of our desire. With one brush of my hand, I cleared the counter so I had room to lean forward and lower my face next to hers.

"I want to watch you, see your eyes when I slide into you." The sound of my zipper seemed to echo around the kitchen as I released my cock and positioned it at her opening. "You're gonna be the death of me."

"Death by orgasm, what a way to go."

"What a way, indeed." I slammed into her, the force of it lifting her feet off the floor and pulling a heated moan from her lips. "God, you feel so good."

She arched her back, and it seemed as if I was diving

deeper into her. With each thrust of my hips, Stella let out a sigh of pleasure, but not once did she lift her hands.

"Tristan," Stella cried out as she tightened and pulsed around me. I pushed deeper, harder, forcing her orgasm higher and higher as my own rolled through me. "Tristan, I love you." With those words, she constricted a little more and I was lost.

STELLA

"This must be yours." I smiled as I handed Tristan the letter and went back to cleaning up the mess. A minute later, I found another letter from the same company, only this one had the telltale yellow sticker on it that listed my forwarding address. They were both from Tander Genetics."

Tristan and I opened our letters simultaneously.

TANDER GENETICS CORPORATION

Stella Elise Lang

Role: Genetic comparison to Tristan Nicholas Christakos

Case reference: LK43P713 Atlanta 05.27

Test Certificate

Following individuals were examined: Stella Elise Lang, Tristan Nicholas Christakos

Regarding the sampling of the participants, please refer to the protocols in copy.

We received the originals of the identity confirmations and of the consent statements.

Method:

Complete autosomal was carried out separately for all samples. Genetic characteristics were determined by comparing 22 numbered chromosomes.

In all analyzed DNA systems:

Minimum cM found: Stella Elise Lang and Tristan Nicholas Christakos 2634.07

Maximum cM found: Stella Elise Lang and Tristan Nicholas Christakos 2941.05

Results are based on the Autosomal DNA segment analyzer used to establish and compare chromosomes 1 to 22 to establish genetic relationship status. The quantitative analysis of the autosomal DNA test shows that the probability of Stella Elise Lang being the direct sibling of Tristan Nicholas Christakos is in the < 99 percentile.

BASED ON OUR ANALYSIS, it is practically proven that Stella Elise Lang is the sibling of Tristan Nicholas Christakos.

I read and reread the letter and studied that fucking centimorgan, cM number, and tried to remember what I had learned at the conference. Genetics had never been an area of interest for me, and although I understood the basics as far as blood types and numbered chromosomes and our one-lettered chromosome getting into the actual similarity percentages confused me. I remembered them saying something about siblings having on average twenty-six hundred or more centimorgans.

I looked up at the chart. No. Just no. There was no fucking way.

"Tristan." I could hear the panic in my voice. This had to be a mistake. "Tristan!"

"Give me a second." He held up one finger.

A second? He wanted a fucking second? No. I was sitting here, his cum still inside me, and was holding a fucking letter that said we were fucking siblings. What the holy fuck? There were no seconds. "Tristan!"

"What!" He inhaled deeply and then tried again. "What?"

The first tear ran down my face. Damn. Damn treacherous tears.

"Don't cry, Stella. There has to be some mistake."

"I'm not crying. I'm not crying. I'm not crying." I had no clue how many times I actually said it, but I stopped mumbling when he reached forward and gently squeezed my hand.

"Let's look at this objectively. We were both swabbed and both tested. So, not only was I tested against you but you were then tested against me, right?"

"I guess. I have no fucking clue!"

I was about to lose it, but he seemed to be holding it together.

"It's sort of like a double-check system. Despite of all of that, there had to have been a mistake, something must have went wrong."

"Really? How? You heard them, and so did I, this is the most comprehensive and accurate DNA test available."

"But, there's no way. My parents have been married for almost forty years."

"Have you ever heard of infidelity? No? I have. Neither of my parents have respect for the sanctity of marriage. It could have been either one of mine."

"But it couldn't have been either one of *mine*. Can you really tell me that you can see either of my parents having an affair?"

"Have you ever seen my mom? She's beautiful. I could so see her coming on to your dad."

His eyes flashed to mine and it was as if an icy chill

123

DANIELLE NORMAN

blasted through the kitchen. Okay, that was probably the wrong thing to say. Wait. No, it was the right thing to say but the wrong way to say it.

"How dare you." He gritted the words through clenched teeth. "My dad has always been loyal to my mom. Plus, your mom doesn't even live here. I've never met her."

"I didn't mean that your dad would initiate the affair, I meant that I can see her hitting on him. She has no shame and would be totally willing to sleep with a married man if she felt like it." I shook my head, trying to straighten my thoughts. "And, as for you never having met her? That doesn't mean your dad never did. She used to live here. It wasn't until after I graduated from high school that she moved. There are plenty of ways she could have run into your dad."

"No. There's no way. I won't believe that. I'll call Tander in the morning and demand they fix this."

We sat quietly, both lost in our own spiraling thoughts. We were still there when the timer on the oven went off. I pulled the lasagna out and set it on the stovetop, not bothering to ask Tristan if he wanted any. If he felt even a fraction of the emotions I felt, there was no way he'd be able to eat.

"We've been sleeping together," I said as I slid onto a barstool. I wasn't sure if he was listening to me or not but there were so many problems that we needed to face. "What if I'm pregnant?"

His stare tracked from where his hands were clenched to where I was sitting. "We aren't related by blood, Stella. I'm telling you that this is a mistake."

"And if it isn't a mistake?"

His lips pinched and his gaze dropped back to his hands.

If it wasn't a mistake, then what were the chances of Carter being related to them as well? What would that do to

124

him and Sophie? It would mean they were first cousins, which still made me uncomfortable to think about.

"It isn't Mana. I know it," Tristan said as he slammed his fist against the counter.

"I didn't think it was."

"It isn't Pops either."

"It isn't immaculate conception."

"What it is, is a goddamn mistake. The lab made a mistake, that's all."

"Yeah, and like I said before, what if it isn't? What if for the last month and a half, you have been sleeping with your half-sister? What if your father cheated on your mom? What if—"

"Stop it, Stella."

"Really, Tristan? Telling me to stop it? This affects me, too. You forget that you aren't the only one here."

"Yeah, but it destroys my parents' marriage, they have forty years invested, we have what . . . a month?"

His words might as well have been a slap across my face. Didn't he get it, this destroys our marriage as well, but obviously, that wasn't all that important to him. "It destroys more than one marriage." My words were soft, almost a whisper.

"Ha, what other marriage? The illegal one? If that test is accurate, you can't honestly tell me that you would want to stay married." He must have seen the look of disgust in my eyes because he continued, "Yeah, me neither. So, why would either of us fight to save this marriage when it never should have happened to begin with when we could fight for one that has lasted for forty years?"

"Fine. So we go to your parents' house and ask them." I slapped my hands onto the counter and went to stand, but before I could, he was on his feet, blocking my way to the door.

"No, we won't. We'll get another test—"

"And, what? Wait another four weeks? That isn't fair." I was mad and hurt and mad—god, I had no clue what I was or who I was.

"Fair? You think it's fair to ruin my family?"

"Not ruin, just ask. We can show them the test results. If Pops tell us this is bullshit, we should still have another test done, but at least we won't be going out of our minds while we wait for the results."

"You don't think my mother will be going out of her mind wondering if her husband had cheated on her and fathered another kid?"

"You think that your wife will be comforted knowing that you might be her fucking brother?"

"Wife? If this is true, we aren't married, which is all the more reason to get the damn second test done. I'm not saying that we shouldn't ever tell them or ask them. I'm just saying that we should be sure before start throwing around accusations."

I hated that he was being so rational. Hated that he couldn't see how scared I was. Hated that he was so willing to brush aside the one thing that might bring me a bit of peace because it might cause his mom distress. And I hated myself for the thoughts going through my head because I loved Christine. But damn it, I needed answers, I wanted them. I deserved them . . . didn't I? I shouldn't have to wait another four weeks while our marriage fell apart.

No wonder people thought I was a bitch, I was acting like one, and I knew it, but in my heart, I didn't care. I needed answers because the man that I thought was my soul mate might be my brother, which sounded even worse than me being a bitch.

"I need to get out of here." I brushed by him, but he caught my elbow and urged me to stop.

"Don't go. We can't discuss this with anyone. We need to pretend everything is normal until we get the new tests."

"Oh, hell no. We deserve some fucking answers."

"No. I mean, yes. Yes, we are going to get answers. Just please let me do the other tests first. I want to call the lab tomorrow. But until then please let me handle it, this needs to stay between us."

"Fine. Call the lab, but don't expect me to sit around and pretend to play the happy wife when you aren't even willing to ask your dad if he fucked my mom!"

"Stella, you're being irrational. Our marriage could very well already be over, why would you risk ruining someone else's?"

"Me? Why would I risk it? You have to be kidding me! I'm pretty sure your dad did that when he fucked around on your mom."

Anger flashed in his eyes, and he stepped back. "If." There was a long moment of silence as he glared, and then he seemed to deflate a bit as he raked his hand through his hair. "Stella, this is important. If we're going to ruin their marriage, then the least we can do is make sure the first test wasn't a mistake."

He just didn't get it. He really, really didn't.

I turned and walked away. The last thing I needed was to be in the kitchen where there were knives and garbage bags and a drawer with duct tape. How fucking dare he. Ruin their marriage? Don't hurt his family? God forbid, we find out the answer and save *our* marriage. He went on and on about that test being a mistake, well, if it was a mistake and he and I weren't related, then I guessed it didn't matter to him. Apparently, our marriage was already over no matter what that second test said.

You know what, asshole, so were bodies.

I strode into the master suite and gathered my nightgown

and toiletries before stomping to one of the guest bedrooms. There was no way I would sleep next to him. Not tonight. Maybe not ever again.

Tristan followed me. "So this is how you're going to play it? It's your way or no way? The world doesn't revolve around you, Stella, there are other people that matter in this world, why are you being so selfish?"

I snapped my attention to him. If he didn't see the flames shooting out of my nostrils then he was in for a shock. "Selfish? How the fuck is stepping away from you being selfish, do you even know what that term means? I'm actually trying to think of others including you."

"Yeah, but not my family."

"I am your family or was until a few minutes ago. Amazing how fast you seem to forget that."

"No, you still are my family, you just might be my sister instead and I have a fucking problem with that." He huffed out several lungfuls of air. "You said it yourself, your mother holds no value for loyalty or marriage."

"And neither do you." My words were soft and if he'd heard me he didn't say anything. "Just leave me alone." I sat on the bed and leaned back.

The picture hanging on the wall rattled as Tristan slammed the door on his way out. I lay there, staring up at the orange-peel pattern of the ceiling. Was that the refrigerator I heard, all the way back here . . . no, maybe it was the air conditioner. I'd never realized how many noises a silent house made.

I curled up as tightly as I could, maybe if I was strong enough, I would be able to keep myself from falling apart and my heart from shattering.

My tears only came faster, soaking the pillow as I watched the numbers on the clock slowly tick by.

Why was it when you closed your eyes and wanted to go

to sleep, you couldn't? Instead, horrid images flashed through your mind, images that you knew would keep you awake for hours. Long lists of what-ifs that were almost wholly improbable but plagued you just the same would form, keeping your imagination running and running and running.

Tears grew heavier as I continued staring at the clock, eleven forty.

Images of Tristan and his family blaming my mother and me. Sophie and Carter splitting because she blamed Carter's family for ruining her family. Ariel taking Kayson's side, Leo being torn between our friendship and her husband, Katy seeing this from only a mother's perspective and not wanting her family around me.

My eyes were still focused on that damn bedside clock, the red numbers displaying two nineteen in the morning and there wasn't a single realistic idea in my head. No, I'd officially lost it. I was a full-force, crazy-ass mental case. I slid from the bed and pulled my clothes on as quietly as I could.

Creaking open the door, I peered out and then held my breath as I listened.

Tick, tick, tick. Mantel clocks, I was never going to own a mantel clock, they were way too loud.

Tiptoeing toward the garage, I picked up my purse on the way and then looked at the alarm panel. In all of our anger, Tristan hadn't set it. Finally, something would be quiet in my escape.

Saying goodbye to the house that was mine for a month, goodbye to the man who I had loved for two years, and goodbye to everything that was almost within my grasp that was until...always until. Until something else happened, until someone better came along, until shitty news landed on your doorstep.

I slipped from his house and didn't look back.

TRISTAN

I'd gotten all of an hour's worth of sleep last night. Every time I reached over to pull Stella into my arms, the cold unmarred half of the bed made everything from last night wash over me. There'd been times in medical school that I thought that I was drowning in work between school and internship but this drowning was different. Back then, I could still breathe, but after last night? It was as if I would never breathe again.

I pulled myself out of bed and got ready for work, if I didn't already know that we were down a doctor, I'd call in. Turning the shower on as hot as I could muster, I let the stream hit me. Each bead of water felt like a thousand needles, but I welcomed the sensation, needed it because this pain was better than the pain in my chest. Resting my head against the shower door, I racked my brain to figure out how my life had gotten so fucked up so fast. One letter, in one afternoon, and it blew everything to fucking shreds.

Before I left the house, I walked down the hall to the guest bedrooms and stood outside the one Stella was sleeping in, but the door was closed. Pressing my ear against the solid wood, I strained to hear something, anything, but there was nothing.

"I love you," I whispered to no one.

I left my house in a daze, barely remembering the drive to work. When I saw how slow the unit was, irritation bloomed in my chest. If it had been hectic, at least my mind wouldn't have been able to wander to Stella and the clusterfuck that was going on in our world. But with nothing exciting going on, it gave me time to think about it all, to read and re-read the letter from Tander Genetics. Waiting until their offices opened was enough to have me pacing, but they were on Pacific time, so I had no choice.

At ten o'clock, I made the call.

"Thank you for calling Tander Genetics. Please listen carefully, as our menu options may have changed . . ."

Oh, god, I hated this, whatever happened to good old customer service?

"Say or press one if this is a hospital . . ." I listened as the automated voice went through each number. "Say or press four if you have received a letter from Tander Genetics and have questions—"

"Four."

"I'm sorry, I did not understand your reply. Say or press seven if you'd like to hear these options again or press zero at anytime for an operator."

What the hell? Why didn't they just tell me that option to begin with? I pressed zero.

"Thank you for calling Tander Genetics. Please listen carefully, as our menu options may have changed . . ."

Really? Was I on some show called *Let's Fuck with Tristan's life*? Ignoring all the options, I pressed four instead of trying to say it and hoped for the best. If not, next time, I'd just start hitting numbers. The line clicked and then music started.

That went on for ten minutes before another click sounded and my call was connected.

"Lab results."

"Hi, my name is Dr. Christakos, and I recently had some tests done through your company via the Genetics Medical conference in Las Vegas."

"Do you have a case number?"

"Yes, mine is LK43D819 Atlanta 05.27"

"Give me one second please."

I waited, my heart pounding as I listened to the stupid music on the other end. My desk drawer was rattling. When I realized it was from my knees bouncing and hitting them thanks to my nerves, I got up and started pacing.

"Dr. Christakos. I have your results in front of me. What may I help you with?"

"Have you had any recalls of your notices? Any equipment malfunctions?"

"No, why?"

"My results cannot be accurate."

"Doctor, there is always that point zero, zero, zero, nine percent chance that we are wrong."

"No, there has to be a mistake. The report you sent me says that some woman who just so happens to work at the hospital where I work is my sister. There is no chance of that being accurate."

"We can send you a kit for a second test. We will need each of you to swab the insides of your cheeks and supply a strand of your hair. I can include a few extra specimen kits, as well. It is even better if you can collect samples from your parents and any other siblings. How many extra kits would you like me to send?"

I took a second to think and then cleared my throat. "Please send a total of eight, which would include the two for us."

"I will send them to this address on Pente Loop?"

"Yes, please." I disconnected and then rested my head on my desk. I had no clue how I was going to get samples from my entire family, let alone bring this up to my family.

The next call I made was to Stella, but it went straight to voice mail. I hung up and decided to go see her down in the ER since she was working today as well.

I took the stairs instead of the elevator, the extra steps would give me some time to think about what to say. Somehow saying, "*Stella, I love you, I miss you. This is a mistake, and you know it will get fixed,*" didn't seem to be strong enough.

"Sorry to interrupt," I said as I approached the nurses' station in the ER, "but is Stella around?"

"Stella called in sick not more than ten minutes ago."

The nurse was looking at me with something akin to bewilderment, obviously confused as to why I, Stella's newlywed husband, didn't know that his own wife was sick.

"Thanks. I was on a call with a lab, and she kept calling, I thought I'd just come down here and see what she wanted, I guess I know what it is now." I gave the nurse a wide smile before heading back up to my office.

When I got there, I tried to call her again, and again, I got her voice mail.

The rest of the day felt as if it were sucking the life right out of me. I hated being at work. I needed to get home and just see her, talk to her, something. Six o'clock couldn't get here fast enough. As soon as Dr. Ahmendel arrived, I was out and heading across town.

Something in the back of my mind wasn't sitting right. I couldn't place my finger on it, but I'd always trusted my instincts, and right then, they were trying to prepare me for the worst. I had no idea what kind of mood she would be in when I got home, but I knew it wouldn't be good.

What would I find when I opened the door? Pressing the remote control to the garage, my ominous feeling intensified when I spied Stella's Mustang missing. Then images from this morning flashed in front of my face. My car in the driveway. Just mine. She hadn't been sleeping when I left; she'd already been gone, and she hadn't come back.

I ran inside, and there seemed to be a hollowness in the room.

"Stella." But I knew it was of no use. Heading into our bedroom, the first thing I noticed was that her trunk was missing. I wasn't sure how she'd gotten it out of here, but it was gone. The beat of my heart seemed to get heavier, and a stone seemed to lodge in my throat as I pulled the door open to our closet and saw all of her stuff gone.

There was no point in checking the bathroom. I knew that it, too, would be cleared out. In one day, she'd managed to empty the house and remove all traces of herself. From the looks of it, you'd never know that she'd ever lived here.

Wiping my hands down my face, I sat on the edge of the bed. What had she done? Why didn't she trust me enough to handle this? I was working on it, but because I was unwilling to jump to accuse my father of cheating on my mom without solid proof, she just bolted?

I called her, but it went straight to voice mail. "I just got home, I see that you've decided to end us instead of sticking it out until we discover the truth. Never pegged you for a quitter, but then again, it seems that my judgment has been way off on a lot lately. The lab is sending us new kits. They are also sending us kits for my parents as well as our brothers. Even though you've abandoned us, can you at least do your part when the tests arrive and give a sample?" I hung up.

"*H*ey, beautiful, you okay?"

I looked up and inwardly groaned. Dr. Wannabee Dreamy was standing next to me. "Fine."

"I noticed that you aren't wearing your ring. Did you come to your senses and realize that you are too much woman to be tied down to one man?"

I tilted my head slightly to the left and then slightly to the right.

"Is everything okay?"

"Yeah, I'm just trying to figure out if you will go away if I throw a stick."

The asshole left, and I returned to entering information from charts into the computer and singing quietly under my breath. "Pah-rum-pum-pum . . ."

"Oh my god, are you singing Christmas carols? It isn't even Halloween."

I sang a little louder. Maybe these nosy freaks would leave me alone. "I have no fucks to give, pah-rum-pum-pum . . ."

"Stella, that isn't really appropriate at work."

I didn't bother to look up. I'd been sleeping on a fucking blow-up mattress that I'd taken from Carter's garage, and I hadn't had more than three hours of sleep any night since moving out of Tristan's house a week ago. These fuckers were going to harp on me, I thought not.

"You know what I don't think is appropriate? I don't think the way you go outside for a smoke break every hour for fifteen minutes when I only get a break every four hours is appropriate. You want to know what else? I don't think it's fair that we have to put up with the same shit every day—I'm not a verbal punching bag, I'm a nurse. Being called a cunt, a bitch, and every other name a patient can think of just because I'm not giving them the medicine that they believe they deserve. Yet, the hospital does nothing, they tell me to take it, and I do. Now, I'm trying to do my job, by myself, and you come over here right after Dr. Never-Going-To-Be-Dreamy bothers me and give me your opinion of what's appropriate . . . no, just no."

Her expression almost made me feel guilty for yelling at her. It wasn't her fault I was losing it. "I'm sorry, Joan, I'm on edge."

"It's okay, we will talk about all of this later. I just came by to tell you that your husband is waiting over by the break room for you."

I cringed when she said *husband*. Telling myself to stay strong, at least in front of my coworkers, I headed to find Tristan, and my heart stopped when I saw him. He wasn't looking my way, and for a few seconds, I stood there and took him in. My arms ached to reach for him and wrap around his body, which fit perfectly against mine. My mind was playing tricks on me, I knew that I wasn't close enough to smell him, but I knew he would smell of cinnamon and peppermint, as if he couldn't decide which he liked better so he alternated. I never asked him if that was what he did, I just always took it for granted.

Shaking my head, I straightened my shoulders and righted myself before I took the last few steps. "Joan said that you needed to see me."

Tristan's face showed no emotion, so I had no idea if he was happy to see me or if he missed me at all. He was more realistic than fairy tales, and at the very moment, probably more controversial than politics when his eyes finally landed on my hand. Tristan's stoic facade crumbled when he realized that I wasn't wearing my rings. I tried to hide it by sliding my left hand into my pocket, but it was too late.

"I got the genetic kits in. I just need to swab your cheek and get a strand of your hair." The temperature in the hospital must have dropped twenty degrees simply by Tristan opening his mouth. His voice was frost and spikes of ice.

I twisted the knob and opened the door to the break room, which was empty since most of the staff preferred the cafeteria. "No one is in here."

"After you." Tristan held the door open and followed behind me. His moves were scientific and analytical with no feelings as he opened the first bag that he'd marked Stella Elise Lang Christakos.

Seeing my name written in his penmanship might as well have been a knife that he'd just shoved into my barely beating heart.

He opened two containers and then snapped on a pair of rubber gloves. I watched him as he collected the sample of my saliva, dropped it into a container, and then sealed it. He was just as meticulous as he collected my hair sample, and when he was sealing the container, he almost made it a point not to look at me.

"I've already gotten my parents and our brothers, I did

that this morning. I told them that we were trying to build a database, and since we were done at the conference, we'd start with our families first. I'd appreciate it if you stuck with that story for now."

I raised one brow. Did he really think I would talk after having stayed silent about it this long? I hadn't talked with anyone—in fact, I'd been intentionally avoiding everyone.

"I know that you don't necessarily hold commitments to the highest standard, but can you at least keep your word and let me handle this?"

I made it a rule to never cry in front of people, but I was on the verge of breaking down.

"Aren't you going to say anything?" Tristan waited for my answer.

"Really? You want me to talk now after you've stood there and said horrid things about my character? You have to be fucking kidding me."

"Well, you were the one to leave. What was it said about your mom? From where I'm standing, the apple doesn't fall far from the tree."

"Fuck you." I raised my middle finger to go along with my words. "You're the one who said our marriage was over, I'm just granting your fucking wish."

"Whatever. I don't have time for this. If this proves to be a load of crap, as I suspect it will, then I've already wasted a month on someone who I thought was going to stick with me for better or worse. I have to get to work, results can take anywhere from two to four weeks, but you know that." Then Tristan pulled the door open and let it slam behind him.

I was left alone, which should have been a relief but wasn't. I'd never been claustrophobic, but this room was caving in on me, it was tiny, so friggin' tiny. I needed to get out of there. Fuck, I needed to get out of this hospital.

When I left the lounge, it was with one goal in mind: get

to the administration offices without running into anyone. When I reached Louise Cameron's office, I let out a long breath and then knocked.

"Come in."

I straightened my shoulders and headed in. "Do you have a second?"

Mrs. Cameron stood behind her desk and gestured me forward. "Sure, come on in and have a seat. What can I do for you, Stella?"

I didn't sit. I moved to the window and leaned a shoulder against the wall as I stared out over the parking lot. Some man must have forgotten where he'd parked because he was roaming up and down the rows. I smiled at the idiot, for one second feeling like my old self.

Mrs. Cameron cleared her throat.

"Oh, I'm sorry."

"I assume that you wanted to speak with me about something."

"I can't—I can't stay here and do this. I can't see him." I'd been so strong, but for some reason, sitting here in front of this woman made me lose it. "I can't, please don't make me."

"I'm assuming that you're referring to Dr. Christakos."

I nodded.

"I know that the two of you are married. I'm guessing that things aren't going as smoothly as you'd hoped. Did something happen that has made you afraid?"

I took her words in, oh, shit. "No. Not at all. Tristan would never physically hurt me. We just can't make us work, but I can't stop loving him."

"I see."

I wanted to tell her that she couldn't possibly have the first clue, but I bit my tongue.

"I'm sorry, Stella, if the two of you decide to divorce, then

I see no reason why it should interfere with your work, provided you can keep it civil."

"I need a transfer to Dr. Phillips' hospital if that's possible. It is much closer to where I live." That was a lie since my townhouse had sold, but I was hoping to find something close to there.

Mrs. Cameron looked at me over the rim of her glasses. "Well, this comes as a shock."

"I know, and I'm sorry. But I need this, and I never ask for anything."

"I understand that, Stella, but there is more to it than just transferring you. Right now, you are not eligible for a transfer."

"What? Why?"

"The hospital has a policy that there are no transfer for ninety days after any type of professional development."

I was quiet for a minute before asking, "How many weeks of vacation do I have coming?"

Mrs. Cameron looked at her computer first. "You have twelve days left."

"Can I take them as my two weeks notice? I can't do this anymore. Please."

She must have seen something desperate in my eyes because she nodded. "I'll make it work."

I stood. "Thank you." Tears brimming in my eyes. "Thank you."

"Go on home, Stella."

When I got home, I didn't rest. I opened my laptop and updated my resume. Then I signed on to Monster dot com and searched for registered nursing jobs in Florida, made a list of those I found interesting, and then forwarded them my resume.

Tomorrow, I'd hit the pavement looking for another job.

STELLA

"Noooo," I sat up with the word still ringing from my lips and then curled into a tight ball. With my forehead pressed to my knees, I tried to erase the vivid images that were still in my mind. I'd been having the nightmares for the last ten days, but they were getting more vivid, clinging to me like damned spider webs long after I opened my eyes. They always started out the same way, I was holding a little boy that looked like Tristan, his head was buried against my chest. But Tristan was nowhere around. Then the image would change, and I was surrounded by Tristan's family, and they were all shouting at me as I tried to cover the baby's head to protect him. Then the image would change again, and it would be just the three of us. I was still holding the baby, but Tristan was standing in front of me, his arms stretched out as he tried to take the baby from me, only I wouldn't let him. It was when the baby reached for me that I saw it, his face, the one who was supposed to be innocent but wasn't. My baby's face was cruel and distorted as he ground his sharp little razor teeth back and forth.

That was always when I had woken in a cold sweat.

Slowly, I forced myself to relax and settle back against my pillows.

When I woke next, it was to my landline incessantly ringing. Who the fuck called someone at five o'clock in the fucking morning, I would never know. I pulled myself up and looked around to see if I had left a bottle of water anywhere, but nope, there only an empty bottle of Korbel and a half-empty bottle of vodka.

I was a nurse and during the daylight hours I knew that I'd been on birth control and the odds of me being pregnant were practically nil. I also knew that birth defects from familial relations didn't take this form, but I wasn't exactly in my right state of mind at the moment.

The phone stopped ringing, only to start again. I yanked the phone so hard that I had to recoil to keep from being smacked in the face from the flying cord that I'd ripped from the wall. I was angry, and everything was suffering my wrath, even my phone. "It isn't even six, why are you calling this early?" I snapped.

"I figured that you would be up and getting ready for work. I wanted to catch you before you left, you've been avoiding my calls."

"I quit."

"You what?"

"Actually, I got a new job."

"Where?"

"I don't want to talk about that. What do you need?"

"Besides my best friend back? We need to talk."

"There's nothing to talk about."

"Right, and I'm a fierce black American woman who wears a size four."

More than anything, I wanted to laugh at her preposterous comment since in reality she was barely five-two and eight and a half months pregnant. "Really, there's nothing to talk about. Tristan and I just have a lot of things to sort out. We need time."

"Well, your friends are worried about you. They'd like to see you."

"I know, and I want to see them—"

"I'm so glad you said that because we're meeting at Sixes at noon. I can swing by at eleven thirty and get you and we can go together."

I groaned. "Fine, I'll come, but I'm driving myself. I have some shit to do this morning."

Ariel didn't say anything, and I knew she didn't believe me.

"I'll be there, I promise."

When I hung up, I forced myself into the shower and then spent the next few hours searching for apartments close to where I'd accepted the new job. Of course, my brother and friends wouldn't be happy, but the thought of moving there actually made me feel better. I would be away from the shit that had happened, and that was really all that mattered.

At twelve, I pulled into the parking lot of Sixes and inwardly groaned. Everyone, and I meant everyone, was there. When I pulled the heavy wood door open, the day-old stale smell of fried food hit me. I loved Sixes, and normally, it was a place that I came to at least once a week, but I'd been avoiding it and it felt like it had been forever since I'd been here.

"Hey," Vivian called out and waved me over to the table. Of all of our friends she was the most subdued. As the owner of Sixes and a widow, she carried a lot on her own shoulders, in comparison my problems still weren't as insurmountable.

"Hi, gang." I tried to force a smile on my face and be my normal charming, okay smartass self but it wasn't coming naturally. Taking a seat at the table I said hello to the rest of the Iron Orchids, the ones who I'd expect to be there and be

145

nosy—Leo, Piper, Everly, Katy, Sophie, and Ariel. But my shock was Ringo being here, sure he came to family parties but not shit like this. "Hey, Ringo."

"Hey, bitch, how's it hanging?" I cracked a smile.

"What do you want to drink, Stella?" Vivian asked as she held a few empty cups in the air.

"Just some water is fine." She set the drink down and then leaned in to give me a hug.

Okay, none of this shit. I was strong, I was a lioness, and I couldn't be either of those if my friends started being all touchy-feely and shit. While I took several deep breaths, I talked myself into staying strong with my normal life's mantra: you came into this world covered in someone else's blood, you have no problem going out the same way.

Sophie reached over and grabbed hold of my arm and lightly squeezed. "I love you. Carter is worried about you. We are here for you, just talk to us."

I yanked back because, yeah, I couldn't do this. Having their support was hard when what I really needed was to be pushing them away. This wasn't fair, I couldn't tell them. I'd promised Tristan to let him handle it, which left me with no option other than to lock my friends out because I didn't have a poker face, not around them. This wasn't fair. I'd never let them lock me out.

"Stella, what is going on? First you and Tristan are happily in love, you move in, it's all a whirlwind, and then, just as fast, you move out. Neither of you are talking to anyone. Tell us something, if we can help, we will." Leo was always the practical one.

"Let us help you fix it." Katy always had that champion attitude, believing we could do anything and get anything done.

For the first time since I sat, I met each of their eyes and studied them for a second before speaking. "I hate to break it to you, but what has happened between me and Tristan can't be fixed."

"But—"

"No buts, Ariel." I shook off whatever she was going to say.

"There has—" Katy cut in.

"No, there doesn't."

"But the two of you—"

I turned to Sophie, her words piercing me the most because, yeah, the two of us had been . . . well, perfect for a month. For one month, I had everything I'd ever wanted, but it was like holding water. You knew you couldn't hold it there forever, it was going to eventually seep out and you'd be left with nothing.

"You are my best friends, and I hope that what I'm about to tell you will stay between us." They all nodded, but for the first time, I seriously doubted their ability to keep this to themselves. "There is no us, and if Ariel hasn't mentioned it yet, I might as well. I'm no longer working at the hospital." I cracked my knuckles and saw Ariel and Sophie cringe. "Soph, I was going to call and see if I could stay with you and Carter just for two nights."

"Of course you can, you know that. Just tell me when . . . shit, never mind, I don't care when, just come on."

"Closing on my townhouse is next week so I need a few days while I get situated somewhere new."

"Of course, you can stay with us. But, if you're having second thoughts, can't you tell the buyers that you changed your mind or something?" Sophie asked.

"At this point, if I backed out, there could be some huge penalties. But . . . honestly, I don't want to. I think it's a sign that my townhome sold so fast. Besides I already have a new place."

"You do?"

I nodded.

"Where are you moving to?" Ariel asked, but the look on her face told me that she knew it wasn't going to be good.

"I've accepted a job at the oncology center at Wolfson Children's Hospital."

"I've never heard of that hospital, where is it?" Ariel asked.

"Jacksonville."

"Jacksonville, what the fuck, Stella? You won't even be here when my baby is born. You're my best friend, you're the baby's godmother, and you throw it on me that you're moving three hours away as if it's nothing. I'm due any fucking day. You've left your husband—who just so happens to be my brother-in-law—what the hell, we are as close as it comes and you're keeping us in the damn dark. I don't get it. Tell us something. This isn't like you. What is wrong?"

"Nothing—or rather, nothing—that I can talk about."

"If I didn't know Tristan better, I'd say that you were acting like a scorned woman." Her comment hit a bit too close to home. Thankfully, she had no idea she was talking about the wrong man being unfaithful. "Holy shit, Stella, what's that look on your face? Is Tristan having an affair?" Ariel threw her hand over her mouth.

"I'll cut his balls off," Leo said.

"You won't have to because Pops will beat you to it and his brothers will hold him down," Sophie answered for everyone. "But I don't believe it, it isn't Tristan." Sophie eyed me, waiting for my answer.

"No. He isn't having an affair."

"Are you?" Ariel asked, suddenly looking at me as if I were a total stranger.

"Really? I've been in love with Tristan since the moment I laid eyes on him. How many men have you seen me date since I decided that Tristan was the one for me? None. So no, there isn't anyone else."

"Then what gives?" Vivian asked, for the first time jumping into the conversation. It made me realize that she and Ringo had been extremely quiet this whole time. "I can't speak for the others, but I know for sure that, if I had the chance to spend time with Mike again, there is no misunderstanding that could keep me away. Nothing makes you realize how precious each day you get to spend with your lover is than when you have no days left to spend with them."

I turned to see if blood and guts were spread across the wall behind me because I wasn't sure if an actual gunshot could have done more damage. It was like, *POW*, right there in the middle of the bar while eating sliders and wings, I knew that my heart quit beating. I was going to literally die from a broken heart. It had a giant hole in it, and I couldn't take this any longer. I loved him so much, and he knew that this was torturing me. Tristan wanted to stay quiet about this to protect his family. Me? I was his disposable commodity.

"I remember when I was younger and hadn't come out to my friends and family that I was gay. Everyday was a battle just to get out of bed . . ." Ringo had started talking, to no one in particular, just talking, but everyone stopped to listen. "I'd ask myself, is today the day that I was going to fight for me or was I going to lay down and take it again? For years, I hid my true identity. I knew with every cell of my body who I truly was, but I couldn't tell anyone. Until one day, I looked in the mirror and the person looking back at me, I didn't recognize. He was a shell, the eyes were cold and showed no emotion—hell, I'd been hiding my true emotions for so long that it had become a habit. Everything about this person looking back at me was calculated and false. That person in the mirror was a cold blooded killer."

Ringo had killed someone? I must have been wearing my

shock for all to see because he continued, "Oh, not like you're thinking, not with a weapon but with deception. Every time I pretended to be who I wasn't, every time I hid my true feelings, I died a little bit inside. Eventually, I would have killed my own soul. But I got a wakeup call when I looked in the mirror. Girl, you need to look in the mirror. You are dying inside. You have friends here who want to help and will love you regardless, and yet, you still aren't being truthful."

"I can't." I couldn't be the one to tell his family even though they had every right to know. They should know, they could help him. No one should be going through this alone. He wouldn't be going through it alone if I hadn't left, but that was a truth I refused to acknowledge. My pride wouldn't let me. So, if I couldn't be there for him, the least I could do was keep my word to wait for the other test results in four fucking weeks.

I needed to get out of there, so I pulled out a twenty and threw it onto the table. Sliding my chair back too fast, it tumbled over, but I didn't stop to pick it up. The only thought on my mind was to get out, get out of there fast.

TRISTAN

For ten days and twenty hours, I'd been going through the motions. I'd sent the samples back to the lab and had marked them urgent, but it was still a waiting game. A waiting game that we had to play while my marriage fell apart. A marriage to the love of my life, a woman who could also very well be my freaking half-sister. It wasn't fair. I sounded like a kid claiming something wasn't fair when I saw in my line of work just how unfair life could be.

When my phone vibrated, I checked to see who was calling, and my heart lifted before plummeting over the fact that this couldn't be good news when I saw Stella's name on the screen.

"Hello, Stella."

"Tristan, do you have a second?" Her voice sounded broken, and I would have done anything to give her what she wanted just to make that tone go away.

"Yeah, anything."

"I can't do this anymore. I've given you time to talk with your family, and you haven't. I need to talk with someone."

"You can talk to me."

Stella's forced laugh only pissed me off. "No, I can't. At one time, I thought that I'd discuss anything with you, but not now. I know where I stand with you. My friends think I'm a horrid person. They think the separation between you and me is all my fault."

"Well, you did move out."

"Don't you dare, Tristan Christakos. You don't get it, and that's fine, but I've been in love with you for so long, and you willingly let it go without a fight."

"Fight? How was I supposed to fight? I called the lab, got new tests, I asked you to stay, but you left and I don't control how fast a lab works."

"Never mind, you don't get it. The bottom line is my friends think I'm the bad person. They think I'm the one that's ruined our marriage. You're making all the rules about when things can be discussed, and to who but I'm the one that comes out looking like a royal bitch. It isn't fair."

"Well, if you'd stayed then no one would have been any the wiser. But no, you are the one who left. You decided to quit our marriage before we had the second results. Results that I believe will prove that we aren't related. You want to be the quitter, fine, so be it, that's your prerogative."

"Asshole."

"Stop calling me names."

"Well, if the shoe fits. You said it wasn't worth ruining someone else's marriage, which meant ours was already destroyed. You said that, not me. Get your facts straight."

"But I didn't leave, until that moment things were still able to be fixed we just needed the results. You called it quits."

"I quit? What fucking marriage? Besides, marrying your sibling is illegal so that blew our marriage out of the water. And if that didn't, the moment you . . . never mind."

"No. The moment I what?"

"Nothing. It doesn't matter."

"It does to me."

"It shouldn't because, even if the results are negative, you made your choice."

"Stella, I don't know what is wrong with you, but do me a favor . . ."

"Hhmm." Exasperation laced her voice.

"Keep your word, you owe me that."

"I owe you nothing." Stella slammed the phone down on me, which was pretty much what I expected her to do.

My phone beeped, and I pounded the speakerphone button harder than I needed to. "Yes?"

"Dr. Christakos, this is Louise Cameron, when you get a second, can you come see me in my office?"

"Absolutely, give me about ten minutes." I let go of the button and slid my fingers through my hair. And it just keeps getting worse.

I checked in with the nurses' station in the neonatal ward before heading down to the admin offices and making my way to Mrs. Cameron's office. It felt like a lifetime ago that I was sitting here with Stella and thought that we would have the time of our lives.

"Dr. Christakos, thank you for making time for me. I'll try to make this fast. As I'm sure you're aware, Stella quit . . ."

She what? What the hell?

"I take it from your reaction that you didn't know this."

I shook my head.

"A few days ago. That isn't why I called you down, though. I wanted to inform you that we are moving forward with the genetics research center and have a few seminars that we'd like you to attend. The only problem is that—"

I finished her sentence for her since it seemed she was taking way too long to get to it. "I need an assistant."

"Yes. You don't have to decide now, but please think about it and let me know."

"I will, thank you." I exited the office, my mind moving at negative ten miles an hour as I pulled my phone out and called Stella. Yeah, I wasn't processing any of this. Not only had my wife left me but also she was giving up her career? To top it off, my family was going to fucking fall apart once all of this got out.

"What?"

"Hello to you, too."

"Well, our last conversation didn't go so well, have you called back to continue destroying me?"

"No. I've called to find out why you quit the hospital?"

Stella let out a long exasperated chuckle as if I just said the most idiotic thing. "I quit because I can't stand being in the same building as you. It is all a reminder of you; you're everywhere. I can't even be around my own brother because his wife is your cousin and, damn it, if she doesn't look like you with that olive skin and those dark eyes. My three best friends are married to your brothers. My job is where you work. I need space—I need to find my own space in the world that has nothing to do with you."

"You don't have to do this."

"Yes. Yes, I do. I really, really do. Listen, I have to go. Let me know when you hear back from the lab, will you?"

"Sure."

Stella hung up, and this time, there was something so final in that click. I pulled my phone back and peered at the black screen. The symbolism wasn't lost on me.

Pulling the door open to my parents' house, I hollered, "Hey, Mana, it's me."

"*Moro mou*, what a surprise. Come in, come in, I just pulled out some *tiropita's* from the oven, want one?"

I grabbed one of the flaky cheese-filled pastries and took a bite as I basked in my mother's presence. She had always made me feel safe and loved and now more than ever I needed that. "Is Pops here?"

"Yeah, he's out in the garage, he and Carter are fixing something for Harlow. Want me to get him?"

I shook my head.

Mana read me as if I'd been a billboard in Times Square, she cupped my face and lightly rubbed my cheek with her thumb. "What's bothering you? You have a lot on your mind."

"Have you ever thought that maybe . . ." Shit, how did I ask this, I started my question again. "Have you ever worried that maybe, you know, Pops is always going places with his job, have you ever worried . . . I mean, you've been married so long . . ."

"*Moro mou*, is that what happened? Did Stella have an affair? Is that why the two of you split?"

"No. Nothing like that."

"I figured that it had to be pretty serious since you two called it quits and you're a Christakos, Christakos men don't quit their women for any reason."

I knew that she had no clue what her words were doing, but they were shredding me.

"I'm going to go talk to Pops if that is okay?"

"Of course. *Agape mou*." Mana kissed my cheek.

"*Agape mou*, Mana." It didn't matter how old I got, I still like hearing my mother tell me that she loved me.

When I stepped into the garage, it was only Pops. "I thought Mana said Carter was out here with you."

"He was, he just ran home to try something. He'll be back in a few. Come on in and have a seat. I'm glad to see you." I had so much anger inside me, and it was all directed at this

155

man. I needed to get it under control. "What's on your mind, son?"

Son. Son? Why did that make my skin crawl? Because when I looked at him, I saw the man who I had always wanted to be, the man who taught me how to fish, how to build things, and told me that I could be anything I wanted as long as I worked for it. He'd bust our asses if we'd misbehaved. There was one time when Damon and I had gotten into trouble for something. I knew that we were going to get a spanking, but I'd watched a movie where the parent had said that when they punished their children, it hurt them more than it did the child so I thought that I'd remind Pops he'd be hurt as well. But it backfired, Pops told me, *"If this hurts me more than it does you, then I'm doing it wrong. Now get your ass over here."* But the man doled out affection just as openly.

"Tristan? You okay?" Pops reached to place a hand on my shoulder and I jerked back. Instantly, I regretted my movement when I saw the hurt in his eyes. "What's going on? You know that you can talk to me about anything."

"Have you ever had an affair?" There, I'd said it.

"What?"

"Have you ever—"

"I know what you said, I just can't believe that you'd even ask that. Not only do you insult me but also you insult Mana."

"It's a yes or no question."

"No, it isn't. It's an are-you-fucking-kidding-me question. How dare you ask me something like that."

"Why so defensive, Pops?"

"Defensive? How about pissed and shocked. What would even make you ask such a thing? Wait, don't answer that. I don't want to know. In fact, I don't want to be in the same room as you right now. Tristan, I get that you're going through something, and I'm sorry for whatever is happening between you and Stella, but you have no right to bring your pain and inflict it in our home." Pops tossed his hands at me. "I can't even talk to you."

"Great, avoid the question because you don't want to answer it."

"No. The answer is no. The answer is that it has never even crossed my mind. Since the moment I met your mother, I knew that she was the only one that I'd ever want for the rest of my life, and no one . . . I mean, no one has ever even come close to holding a candle to her. She is perfect in every way. After forty years of marriage, the woman makes me feel like a newlywed when she smiles at me. I'd do anything for her, which currently includes not killing one of her sons." Pops marched out of the garage and into the house, slamming the door behind him. Hammers and screwdrivers that neatly hung against the wall shook from the vibration.

"Wow, you really screwed that up, didn't you?"

I turned and saw Carter standing at the garage opening, just staring at me. Holding out one hand toward him, I walked past. "Don't, just don't."

"If you think that I'm going to let you walk off that easy, you have another think coming. You've destroyed my sister and pissed off Pops. Am I to assume there are other people as well that you've inflicted your joyful disposition on?"

TRISTAN

*C*arter's fingers tightened as he gripped my upper arm as I tried to pass him. "Oh, no, you don't. You don't get to just walk away. You made me a promise that you'd take care of her, and now she is broken. You're broken, too, and you are taking it out on your dad? What gives?"

"This doesn't concern you. Stay out of it." I yanked free and walked toward my car.

"This is my family, too. It's my sister, my children's aunt, my children's uncle, now you're going after Mana and Pops? Let's just destroy everyone, is that it? Misery loves company."

"Carter, you don't get it."

"Try me."

I opened my car door, and a forceful hand from behind shoved it closed. "Move your hand."

"No, you're going to tell me what is up."

I ground my teeth together, knowing he wasn't going to let it go. "Fine. I'll meet you at my house, I need a drink." Carter let go of my car door, and I hopped in.

Once inside, I changed into jeans and a T-shirt and then walked into my kitchen and reached for a bottle of Macallan.

Not just any bottle, either. I went for the one that I kept reserved for big events, Macallan twenty. Let's be honest this was a big event. I pulled out a couple of glasses and poured myself two fingers over an ice cube.

Carter walked in and eyed the bottle. "Oh, shit," he groaned, finally grasping how big of a fucking deal this really was. "You better give me the same."

I poured his drink and then handed it over. "Have a seat, I'll be right back."

When I walked back into the kitchen, I was holding the letter. "Before you read this, you have to promise me the information goes nowhere."

"I can't promise that." I raised an eyebrow at him, and he shrugged. "A lot of people are being hurt, they deserve to know what's going on."

"They will, everyone will. But if you want to know what's going on, you need to promise that the information stays between us."

Carter huffed and extended his hand. "Fine."

I let him take the letter and then leaned against the wall as he read it.

"What's a centimorgan?"

"It's a unit of measurement only used in genetics."

"This doesn't make sense, there has to be some mistake. You two had just kissed and your saliva was too strong in her mouth, something. This does not make sense."

"It was a blood draw and hair sample, not a saliva swab. But the way your mind works is interesting. I agree that it doesn't make sense."

"Wait, what about me?"

"That's why I came by and got your hair sample and swabbed your cheek. We are having an extensive DNA test done to see who all is affected."

"Are you thinking that it was my dad and your mom?" Carter asked somewhat reluctantly.

I shook my head. "Look at me. I'm the spitting image of my dad. If it weren't for Mana giving birth to us, you'd never know that we had any other DNA but his. All four of us boys look like Pops."

"So, you're saying Pops and my mom?"

I nodded.

"But Stella looks like me, we look like both of our parents."

"Both of your parents are tall, blond, and blue eyed. Technically, it could be either one."

"We both have our dad's chin."

"That is a matter of opinion. I'm not arguing—god, I hope that you are right, but until we know for sure, we can't take that chance."

"I understand the not taking a chance, fine don't sleep together. But couldn't you have at least treaded on thin ice a bit, what happens when this proves to be one giant cluster-fuck, what then? You've totally destroyed everything the two of you had, and there will be no putting it back together."

"Funny how you assumed I was the one who walked. I wasn't. She was. I wanted to wait until we got the new tests. I thought that we'd just sleep in different rooms. Hell, I don't know. I'm disgusted by the thought of sleeping with a sibling, but then I analyze how I feel about Stella, and all rationale goes out the window."

Carter grabbed his head as if trying to hold all of this information in. "Wow, this is a lot."

"Tell me about it. What if it all proves to be accurate? We have to get a divorce without anyone finding out. I mean, I wouldn't care so much about my dad, but my mom? She's innocent. Stella's innocent. If it is an error on the lab's part? I'm not sure it would matter to Stella. She has so much hatred toward me over all of this when all I wanted was to take the proper steps. She just isn't thinking rationally."

I wanted Carter to see what I saw. I was being responsible, doing the mature thing, making the medically sound decision . . . wasn't I?

"Stella's thinking with her heart, have you stopped to ask her what she wants?" Carter took a long swig of his scotch and handed me back the letter.

"She wants to march into Mana and Pops house and demand to know if he slept with her mom." I looked around the room. "I told her that I wanted to wait and be sure before we burned down their marriage, and her answer was to pack her stuff and leave in the middle of the night. Hell, she didn't even bother to leave me a note. I woke up the next morning and thought she was safe in bed. Worse, she even took off her wedding rings." The more I thought about that part, the angrier I got. "She just wants us to tell everyone, ruin everyone's lives before we know for sure whether or not the test was a fluke. Yeah, like a giant explosive that destroys everything so she can move on. She is on a destructive path." I swallowed some of the scotch and relished the burn.

"That doesn't sound like her."

"Then you don't know her." I downed the rest of my drink. Obviously, this conversation was over. "Please just respect what you told me and let's keep this between us. I'm handling it."

Carter nodded and left my house, but I got up and poured me another drink. This time, it was Macallan twelve year.

STELLA

$\mathcal{I}$'d left Sixes almost five hours ago but didn't have the courage to go home. I wasn't sure what I was more afraid of: someone coming by to try to force me to talk, the memories of moving out knowing that I was starting my life with Tristan, or that I'd get tired and fall asleep and have that fucked-up nightmare again.

I only had four more nights in my little house anyway. I drove past Historic Harley Davidson and a pang of loss hit me. Would the girls still consider me an Iron Orchid? I was one of the founding members, wasn't I? They probably would until Tristan found someone new . . . at that thought I had to pull over, I couldn't catch my breath. It hurt, it hurt so damn bad. Clutching my throat, I tried to regain control, but it was no use. I needed to go home.

Putting my car back into gear, I maneuvered it back toward Metrowest, where I lived. When I turned onto my street, I spotted Ariel's car in my driveway, and when I pulled up and cut my engine, she slid from the driver's seat.

"What are you doing here?"

"Waiting for you."

"I thought Kayson didn't want you to drive with the baby due any day."

"The man needs to realize that women have been having babies for centuries, and just because I'm pregnant, it doesn't mean that I've suddenly become an invalid."

"He's at work?" I asked, totally guessing that he had no clue that she'd been driving and that was why she thought she'd get away with it.

"Yeah, he's working late."

"Come on in." I headed up to my door. "Oh, be warned, I didn't unpack my storage unit, so I don't have much in here."

"It's fine." Sure, she said that now but I seriously doubted she'd think that once she saw we had no place to sit except an air mattress on the floor.

"I have some bottles of water in the fridge, want one?" I headed into the kitchen.

"Yeah. Umm, Stella, are you sleeping on that?"

"Yep, it's fine." I handed her the bottle. "I only have two more nights, but then I'll be at Sophie's until I leave."

Ariel took a sip. "Do you have anywhere else we can sit? If I get down there, there is no way I'll ever get back up again."

"Sorry, no." Ariel headed back toward my bedroom, I had no clue what she thought she'd find but the place was empty. She should know since she helped me empty it. But she stopped at the guest bathroom. "Oh, sorry." I stepped back.

"No, come on." Ariel put the lid on the toilet down and sat. "You can sit on the counter." I chuckled at her ingenuity. "What's going on, truthfully?"

"I want to tell you, I do."

"Then tell me. Whatever it is, is killing you. You need to talk it out. I'm your best friend. Please, Stella, talk to me."

"Ariel, I can't. Too many people will be hurt." I buried my face in my hands.

"Being hurt is something we can live with. Dying from

keeping this inside isn't. I'm not willing to lose you just so a few people don't get butthurt."

"It's more than that. It will hurt everyone."

"You mean me?" Ariel pointed to herself, looking totally confused.

"Yes, but it will really hurt Kayson, Damon, and Ian. God, it will kill Christine." I rolled my head from side to side trying to alleviate some of the stress that I'd been carrying. "I probably should wait until we know for certain."

"No." Ariel's words were crisp and adamant. "This is destroying you and our family. You'll tell me now, and we'll make a plan. Let's talk through it, I'm here for you and we are going to find a solution."

I shook my head. "There's no solution. I've tried to come up with some answer."

"What about Tristan? Does he know?"

I nodded.

"How does he feel?"

"He's hurt, but he's made his opinion known."

"What opinion is that?"

"To protect his family." I pulled my leg up and rested my arm on my knee. Biting my thumbnail, I thought about everything that had happened. "When I was little, it didn't matter what I told my mom, if her latest boyfriend told her something different, she'd take his side. In school, if some rich bitch did something, I'd put that last-season-Prada-wearing preppy in her place. But I was the one who got into trouble. Now, when I feel that this could be resolved much faster by just talking to certain people, Tristan wants to handle it because it's more important to save his family than it is to possibly save ours." I wiped away the few tears that had streamed down my cheeks. "Once, just once, I want someone to say, 'I'm on your side, Stella. I'll stand up for you.'"

"I'm on your side, Stella, but I need to know what your side is so I can also stand up for you."

"Do you remember when we were having our *Sons of Anarchy* marathon and there were those few episodes where Jax went to Ireland? We all about died when we thought that he and Trinity were going to make out. You all were all cringing and covering your faces because we knew that Trinity was his half-sister?"

Ariel nodded, trying to understand my words. "You threw a fit."

"Yeah, because I couldn't understand how you all sat there and watched these men kidnap and kill people, gang rape women, and sell drugs, but couldn't stand the thought of him making out with his half-sister."

"Okay. Now, I'm really confused." Ariel shook her head. "Is Tristan selling drugs?"

I shook my head.

"Just tell me, I can't imagine there being anything that perfect Tristan would do that was comparable to *Sons of Anarchy* or that he'd put before his marriage vows. Come on, look at his dad."

I cringed at that last part . . . his dad. My dad? No, it just didn't feel right.

"Let me help you, Stella. I love you like a sister. Hell, we *are* sisters."

I didn't say anything at first because she needed to understand how big my secret was while she still had time to turn around.

"We are sisters," she said again. "Nothing you say is going to keep me from helping you. Besides, if this involves the family, then who the hell does Tristan think he is keeping it from everyone? Sounds like Tristan has a bit of a God complex going on."

I buried my face in my hands, having finally reached my breaking point.

"Please." Ariel's simple one word plea shattered me.

"Maybe you're right, maybe Kayson and the others should know." Letting out a long, pent-up breath, I went for it. "You know how Tristan and I had our genetics done while we were in Vegas?"

"Yeah?"

"We got the results back."

"And?"

"And ... well ... it's bad."

"How bad?"

"I'll be back." I held up one finger and then headed to the living room to where I'd been sleeping. Pulling the folded letter out of its envelope that I'd kept hidden between the mattress and the fitted sheet, I took it back to the bathroom. "Here." I shoved it toward her.

"What is this?"

"Just read," I said a bit too forcefully, and it took her a minute to look from me to the paper in her hand. As if, somehow, she knew that doing so really would change everything.

"This doesn't make sense, there's no way."

"Right? That was what we said. But they ran our numbers twice, mine against Tristan's and then Tristan's against mine. Both times, they came up with the same conclusion ... we're related and not just related distantly—he's my half-brother. I'm his half-sister. We've committed incest." I threw my hand up against my mouth as my stomach started to churn. "We are assuming that is was Pops and my mom."

"If this is true, and I don't think it is, this is going to destroy Christine."

"I know, right? Now you understand why it's killing me?"

"Stella, god, I'm so sorry, sweetie. I had no clue that you were carrying all of this on you." Ariel reached out but all she could touch was my ankle so she clasped on. "My heart is hurting for all of you. You shouldn't have had to carry this all alone. That's what sisters are for, we lighten the burden. Tristan should know this better than anyone, he has great brothers."

I tucked my head between my knees and stared down into the sink. It was weird how your mind wandered to weird shit at times like this, like how gunky the drain looked, and whether or not that was hard water build up around the spigot.

"I don't feel that I should keep this from Kayson. Please tell me that you understand this."

Those words had me instantly looking up.

"At the very least I think that you should talk to Carter, he's your brother after all. If George and your mom did have an affair, was it just once? Are you the only child he has that Christine doesn't know about? What about Carter? Who's his dad? Hell, are he and Sophie first cousins?"

"I don't know, I don't know, I don't know." I grabbed onto the roots of my hair and tugged. "Tristan got more genetic tests for us and the rest of the family as well, we are just waiting for the results."

"How long?"

"Weeks . . . can be four."

"So, is it worth being all Chicken Little and the sky is fall-ing? Should you wait until you know for sure?"

"It doesn't matter, it's so much more than just the results now. Tristan gave up on us. He threw our marriage under the bus the moment he decided that we were going to wait to talk to his parents until after we got the second tests back. He was more concerned about what it would do to them than what it was doing to us. I love George and Christine, I do, but I needed to know whether or not there was any truth to these results. He expected me to pretend everything was hunky-fucking-dory." I chewed on my thumbnail, a horrid habit that I'd started in the last week. "In one breath he had said the test was wrong and in the next he had said our marriage was over. He might as well have said, *I don't care, I'm done with you, Stella. You aren't worth it, no one would want to go through this shit and still stay married to you.*" I plopped my feet into the sink, my butt on the counter, and buried my head against my knees. "I felt like he was blaming me for everything, all his anger over this mess had him blaming it on me and our marriage. I get it, I do. If we were half-siblings, then this whole thing was totally gross. But my brain knew that this had to be false. If George had slept with my mom, why would he support having me around his family? Or Carter, for that matter? The last thing he would want is to open a pathway where our mother would come back into his life, right?"

Ariel nodded. "Tristan needs help."

"I know he does, but he thinks he has to handle it all. And I'm of no help, my heart is just broken by all of this. For all I know, my whole life has been a lie. The one man I thought I was in love with is the one man I can't be in love with. All my life, I've been the loud one—I know that. I wanted to see everyone get their dues, good or bad. I always thought that mine would come in time, you know?"

Ariel kept silent and let my emotions pour.

"But this . . . what did I do that was so wrong? Sure, I can be a bitch but only to people that truly deserve it. I'm never mean just for the hell of it, you know that, don't you?"

I glanced up at Ariel and she nodded. "Of course I do."

"I just wanted him to stand up for me and say, 'if there's any hope for us, we can't put this off another second. But he didn't. Instead…I don't know…what was my point?" I wiped the tears from my face. "Oh, yeah, Tristan never saw me as a prize . . . well, maybe a prize from the gumball machine. But I'm worth more, at least I want to be worth more."

"Oh, Stella, I'm so sorry. You are priceless. Why do some men have to suck?"

"And not suck in a good way?"

"Please let me talk with Kayson, maybe he can talk with Tristan, and if they decide to go to Pops, then he is probably best anyway. Of all of them, he's the one that's actually had training for how to handle and deliver bad news, you know the whole cops appearing in the middle of the night."

"Yeah, okay, I don't think Tristan can hate me anymore than he does now and maybe this can help him."

EVERYONE THINKS THEY CAN TELL JUST ONE PERSON

Ariel

I moved the pork chops to the skillet I'd been slow cooking tomatoes in for the last two hours. Kayson still loved his Greek food, but he'd also acquired a fondness for some of my Southern home cooking. Tonight, I decided to cook his favorite. We needed to talk, he needed to know what was going on. Tristan shouldn't have to handle this alone just like Stella shouldn't have been asked to stay quiet. But, Christ on a cracker, how was I supposed to broach the subject? I had sat on this since yesterday and gone back and forth over the whole should-I-or-shouldn't-I-tell-him thing.

Did I just let it fly and say, *"By the way, thirty-two years ago your dad may have had a tryst with Stella's mom, and guess what . . . you have a sister?"*

Nah, I'd better not. Maybe I should write it in a letter. Or embroider it on a pillow or cross-stitch it. Okay, I was seriously losing it.

What if this wasn't true, what if it was all a big mistake? Did I just keep my mouth shut and leave Stella and Tristan to go through it alone, call them casualties of war? No. I knew better than that, in fact I'd seen proof to the opposite of that. We were stronger together. Tristan needed his brothers. Whether true or false they needed to be united not just for each other but if it was true then for Christine. And Stella needed us . . . her . . . gang. I heard Stella's voice in my head. "We've got ourselves a gang." That was what she needed, she needed us around her to support her.

"Hey, Sweets, dinner smells wonderful," Kayson said as he walked in from the garage and dropped his keys on the counter. "Why don't you sit? I can finish this." He rubbed his left hand over my belly and then dropped a soft kiss to my neck. "I'm sure our little guy has exhausted you."

Yeah, being pregnant was a breeze compared to what I was getting ready to lay on him. "No, I'm all right, I'm almost done anyway. Why don't you go change out of your uniform, and by the time you come back down, it will be done."

"Okay. Have I told you how beautiful you look?" He leaned forward and gave me another kiss.

"No." I grinned, and he leaned closer.

"You are the most beautiful woman I've ever seen."

The man spoiled me, and as he headed upstairs, I wanted to follow him. Since I couldn't, I moved quickly—or, as quickly as I could considering I was ready to pop any day—and got the food on the table. When Kayson came back down, I wanted everything on the table so we could both sit and relax. It was going to be a long night.

GUYS GOSSIP AS MUCH AS GIRLS

*K*ayson

    I shoved my hand through my hair as words like *affair* and *siblings* rolled around my brain. "I need to talk to Ian. Do you mind—"

"Go." Ariel waved me off. I was thankful that she understood that I needed to process this, but I needed one of my brothers as a sounding board.

Pulling out my phone, I sent a text to Ian.

ME: You home?

    Ian: Yep. Just finished dinner. What's up?

    Me: Need to talk.

    Ian: My house or yours?

    Me: Mine.

    Ian: Be right over.

"IAN IS GOING to come over here."

"I wanted to get some sewing done anyway, I'll be back in my craft room."

I walked over and held out a hand to help her up then pulled her into my arms. Her kiss was sweet, and at the same time, strengthening. It gave me the encouragement to do what I felt I needed to do. How was I supposed to discuss this with my brother? Part of me was angry with Tristan for not telling us. He shouldn't have kept this to himself or expected Stella to keep this. He should have known that it would get out. It wasn't fair to put this much stress on our wives when we could help them.

I released my hold on her when our front door opened. Ariel headed off to her sewing room, and I moved to the kitchen and grabbed four beers. We were going to need more than one each.

Ian spotted me and blew out a deep breath. "Shit, it's that bad?"

I nodded. Then he followed me to the couch, which was where he sat while I told him everything.

SHHH, WE NEED TO KEEP IT JUST BETWEEN US

*L*eo

I turned off the Hallmark channel, my secret guilty pleasure, when Ian walked in.

"What's wrong?" I jumped up when I got a good look at his face. "You look like your dog just died." Ian shook his head. "Baby, talk to me. What's wrong? Is everything okay with Kayson?" Ian nodded. I threw my hands over my mouth and felt the tears already building, yes I was crying a lot more thanks to pregnancy hormones. "Ariel? Is Ariel okay, what about the baby?"

"Ariel is fine, the baby is fine. It isn't Ariel or Kayson. Can we sit?"

I pulled him to the sofa and sat next to him, wrapping my arms around his waist as I waited. He'd tell me when he was ready. That was the one thing about Ian, he was analytical. Whatever it was he'd just learned, he needed to play it over several times in his mind before he said anything.

We sat on the couch for almost two hours, neither of us saying a word. I'd turned the television back on and when the movie finished, I got up and headed to our room to get ready for bed. I was brushing my teeth when his reflection appeared in the mirror.

"You know that genetics conference that Tristan and Stella went to?" He wasn't asking for me to answer, he was talking it out, this was how he processed, so I nodded and finished my nightly routine quietly. "Well, each attendee had their own genetics done, and it was compared to their teammate. They got the results back a few weeks ago. Stella and Tristan are siblings."

Okay, I totally was confused. "What?"

"I know. I'm having a hard time with this. I don't know if this means that Carter is also related to us or if it is just Stella. Or, is it Tristan who is related to Stella and Carter? I need to take this in. I'm not sure what to do. Tristan came by two weeks ago and took a sample from each of us." I raised one brow, questioning him since I wasn't sure who he was referring to when he said *each of us*. "My brothers and me. Oh, and Carter as well as Mana and Pops. Tomorrow, I want to do a little more research on DNA tests."

I nodded, but that night, I didn't sleep well. The next morning after Ian left for work, I called into my shop and asked my manager to handle things for me. Then doing something I probably shouldn't, I called Katy. I truly wanted to talk to Sophie, but she'd tell Carter, and since he was Stella's brother, I was afraid that it might blow up. But Katy could help in a different way, she'd talk to Damon, and maybe he'd be able to help Ian, who was my main concern.

DID YOU EVER PLAY THE
TELEPHONE GAME AS A CHILD?

*K*aty

"Hey, Bee bug, can you do Mom a favor?"

"Sure."

"Can you go over to Aunt Sophie's and play with Harlow for a bit?"

"Yeah, but why?"

"I want to talk to Daddy."

"Is Daddy in trouble?"

"No, nothing like that."

"Are you sure that Daddy isn't in trouble because I know something that he did?"

"Bee, are you tattling?"

"No. I'm informing for his own safety."

I looked down at my precocious ten-year-old and raised one eyebrow. The balance between teaching her the difference between tattling and what was telling for safety sake had been a challenge.

"Daddy is going to sink our house."

"What? What makes you think that?"

"He and Uncle Kayson were talking, and they didn't know

that I was there. Uncle Kayson said that Daddy must be happy that Maggie is finally six weeks old." I fought to hold back my groan. I had a bad feeling about this. "He told Uncle Kayson that he was going to sink it home."

Sink it home? Aw shit, sink it home.

Got it.

I needed to talk to Damon about what he and his brothers openly discussed.

"Bee, I think you misunderstood."

Bee shook her head "No, he said sink it home."

"Okay, well, I'll talk to Daddy about this, but he was probably talking about the pool, you know, where things sink. You can't really sink a home, can you?" Shit, if anyone overheard this conversation, I'd probably be arrested.

Bee thought for a second and then shook her head, finally seeing my point. "No, that would be hard."

"Yeah, real hard." I bit my tongue to keep from laughing. Sometimes, this parenting thing was difficult to get right. "But you know better than to eavesdrop. That was rude and wrong."

Damon walked in at that moment and Bee ran to him and threw her arms around him, "I'm sorry, Daddy, I didn't mean to eavesdrop."

"Okay." Damon looked over her head for some clarity. I just waved it off. "Just don't do it again."

"I promise." Bee released her hold. "Bye, Mom, I'll be back later." Bee ran out the door and over to play with Harlow.

"Hi, sweetheart, missed you at work today, everything okay with Leo?" Damon walked up and gave me a kiss.

"Yeah, she just had a lot on her mind that she needed to talk out."

"Is Maggie asleep?"

"I just put her down for a nap. Listen, can we talk for a second?"

"Sure, everything okay?" Damon grabbed me by the hand and headed into the living room. He settled into his favorite oversized chair and pulled me onto his lap.

I carefully thought about my words and what to say. I played each one in my mind before I said them.

THREE CAN KEEP A SECRET IF TWO
OF THEM ARE DEAD

*C*arter

This was a giant clusterfuck. I looked at Sophie, who had tears in her eyes, and I couldn't blame her. She'd always thought so highly of her uncle, but me? I wasn't surprised to hear this about my mother.

"You knew this all along and didn't tell me?"

"Soph, please understand."

"I don't, Carter, I'm sorry but I don't. You kept this from me. This involves our family and what . . . you didn't think I deserved to know?"

"That isn't it, and you know it. There are a lot of factors to consider, one being that I was told in confidence, and the second is that we don't have all of the facts. Why in the hell would I put you through this"—I reached forward and wiped the tears off her cheeks—"before I knew the entire story?"

"So, what do we know?"

"Not much. We're not even sure if it is just Stella or if it was both Stella and me. Because you and I both know that it had to be George. There's no way Christine—"

"No. You're right. I can't see Aunt Christine having an

affair with anyone, let alone your dad. Besides, all four boys look exactly like my uncle, so I doubt that Tristan isn't George's."

"I know, which is why I wonder about me. Stella and I look a lot alike."

"But both of your parents are tall, blond, and blue eyed. You and Stella truly look like either one of them."

I wove my fingers together behind my neck and craned my head back. "Does this mean that you and I are related?" Bricks seemed to fall into the pit of my stomach at those words.

Sophie was quiet, but I knew that her mind was working overtime. "It depends on your results. If we are, then we are first cousins, same as I am with Tristan and the rest of them."

"Fuck!"

"I don't care, we're doing nothing about it, we're changing nothing, Carter, do you hear me? I love you. I can't have children anyway. So, it isn't as if we have more genetic shit to worry about."

"Are you okay if I don't hear the results?"

"You don't want to know?"

"Fuck, no. I'm thirty-two years old. I've been okay this long living in the dark, I can live another thirty-two years just as blind."

"But what about your sister? God, this must be killing her."

"It probably is. At least now we know why they split up."

"I'm going to talk to Ian, but I think that we need to call a family meeting and everyone needs to be there," Sophie said, her words were like a final edict. "Uncle George and Aunt Christine need not to be kept in the dark. Stella should not be the outcast for someone else's mistake. If the boys aren't going to do this, then I will."

"Don't you think that Tristan should be the one to call that shot? He is the one holding the test results."

"He should have told us the second he found out, mistake or not. Since he didn't and it doesn't seem like he's going to anytime soon, someone has to. I don't mind being the bad guy."

I knew if I pushed her on this, it would probably blow up in my face, so I nodded and gave her an almost defeated sounding, "Okay."

TRISTAN

"Gee, to what do I owe this surprise?" I looked at the cooler my brothers were holding between them.

"Cut the bullshit, it's time we talk." Damon pushed me back and barged in, the cooler hitting my legs.

"Jesus, what's in that thing?"

"Two cases of beer."

"Why?" I asked as I moved to the living room and took a seat. Damon set the cooler down next to my coffee table and Ian headed into my kitchen and grabbed a bottle opener and garbage can.

"Someone care to fill me in? What's going on?"

"We know," Kayson said nonplused.

"You know? Know what?" I met his gaze and then met the deadpan looks of my brothers. "She told you? She fucking promised to let me handle it. How dare she, I fucking can't believe her, I can't fucking trust anything she says."

"Hold your horses there, Ranger, you shouldn't have ever asked her to keep something like this a secret, it isn't fair. Besides, you should have come to us. We're brothers, we have as much of a right to know as you do.

185

Who do you think you are handling all of this behind our backs and then forcing your wife to carry our fucking burden?" Damon's words were a punch in the solar plexus.

"No one should be expected to shoulder so much, and from the sound of it, you weren't even there for her. My god, no wonder the woman is moving to Jacksonville." Kayson glared at me. "I don't know that Ariel will ever forgive you for this."

"Wait, what? Stella's moving to Jacksonville?"

"Oh, she didn't tell you? Yeah, we knew." Kayson was still glaring as he answered me.

"And I'm just now finding out?"

"Pot meet kettle. How does it feel to be the last one to know something of importance?" Ian asked with disgust. "But we aren't here to talk about you and Stella, I think that you've fucked that up bad enough, and truthfully, she is better off without you."

I'd never wanted to kill one of my brothers as much as I did right then. Damon must have read the emotions roiling through me because before I could leap from my chair, he was holding me down. "Enough, all of you. First thing's first, can you tell us exactly what you know and what you've done so far?"

I grabbed the letter and handed it to him, he read it aloud, and I translated the medical jargon as he went along. "Basically, it all but guarantees she and I are related. I can't see Mana, I just can't."

My brothers all concurred on that statement, at least.

"As hard as it is to believe, I'd have to say Pops."

"I can't believe that either. He's like us—hell, he taught us what it's like to be a man. Have any of you ever even looked at someone other than your wife?" Damon looked at each of us seriously. "Since realizing that you had feelings for Stella have you ever looked at another woman and thought, 'I'd like to fuck her?'"

I shook my head.

"Have you even noticed another woman since you laid eyes on Ariel?"

Kayson shook his head.

"How about you, Ian? Since seeing Leo as more than a friend—"

"Don't need to finish the sentence, the answer is no."

"Exactly, which is why I can't see Pops doing it," Damon reiterated.

"But we're newlyweds, Pops and Mana have been married over forty years." I leaned my head back and rested it on the back of the chair. "I know, I know, no, I can't imagine feeling any different in forty years," I said, totally beating my brothers to their defense.

"So, how do we prove this?" Damon asked.

"We do another test replicating the same situation and then we do a second test where we change one variable." Ian, ever the scientist, had obviously thought about this.

"I've already sent out another round of samples. That was why I collected the swabs and hair samples. I didn't just collect from the three of you but I also gathered from Mana, Pops, and Carter."

"Perfect, when will those results be in?" Ian sounded like a kid at Christmas time.

"They can take two to four weeks, so we should have them back any day."

"We can't wait that long, the family is falling apart, we need answers now," Damon explained. "I think we need to call a family meeting. With everyone, and I mean, everyone."

"Sophie beat you to it, she's already called one," Ian said. "I just thought it might be nice to give you the heads up that you didn't give us."

I finished my first Yuengling, tossed the bottle into the garbage, and then reached for another.

THOSE WHO KNEW, which was basically the majority of us, knew how important this was, and those still in the dark, which was my parents, were curious as to why their children and their children's spouses were gathering for an impromptu meeting. The hardest part was getting Stella to agree to come as well.

At seven o'clock, I walked into my parents' house.

Mana had chairs pulled into the living room, and Damon and Katy were already there. "Hey, where are the girls?" I asked.

"Aunt Dion is watching them so we could have this out," Pops snapped. I turned my attention toward him, but he was looking at Mana, a gentle smile on his face.

I felt her before I saw her. The temperature in the room warmed, and a slightly exotic scent seemed to fill the air. It was signature Stella and her perfume that drove me wild. Maybe I was a lightning rod asking to have the shit shocked out of me but I couldn't refrain from moving close to her and inhaling the exotic fragrance.

I took a seat, and a small part of me cringed when she moved to the opposite side of the room, she never locked eyes with me. Once everyone arrived, it was Mana who actually began.

"I don't like this. All of you are my family, and we've not been together in weeks. The children are hurting, I'm hurting, and now Pops is hurting. Who wants to start and tell me what is going on?" She waited and slowly scanned the room, meeting each person's eyes before stopping on Stella. Mana raised one brow in challenge, and Stella shook her head, so

Mana moved to me. "Fine, then you begin since you seem to have so much to say lately."

"I don't know where to begin." My palms were sweating, and my irritation was growing. This whole fiasco was my brothers' idea, and they were just going to sit by and watch? I didn't want to be here. I didn't want to have this conversation or toss around accusations about things I didn't have verified facts to support. If it were up to me, I would have waited until we had the second round of tests in hand and knew that there was actually something to talk about before we brought the whole family into it.

"How about start with why you believe your father might have had an affair?"

The pain that laced her voice was like a sledgehammer. I was shocked that Pops had told her, especially if it had been true.

I reached into my back pocket, pulled out the letter, and handed it to her. She scanned the contents and then looked at me. "What's this? It makes no sense to me." She handed it back.

"It says that Stella and I are related."

"I know what the letter says, I'm not daft. I want to know *why* you'd even believe it. It is preposterous."

"It's medically proven."

"Really? Show me."

I pointed to the numbers. "These numbers are only found among siblings."

"Fine, and how do you know those are your numbers? You can't tell me that it is medically proven because you weren't there when they ran your samples. All you see is a piece of paper that tells you it's fact. You want to know for sure, then don't send it off to some lab where they probably do hundreds of these a week."

I didn't want to correct her and say more like thousands a

day, but I understood her point. "I know, and if you remember, I got more samples from all of you and had sent them off."

"To the same incompetent lab that did this?" Mana tapped her toe, waiting for an answer.

"Yes, they offered."

"And why do you think they were so willing to re-do the tests? They realized they were idiots."

"Which is why I didn't want to bring this up to you until we got the second set of results."

"You doubted the results?" Damon looked perplexed. "Then why in the hell have you been creating so much drama?"

"What the hell, man, I'm not the one that's been creating drama, I've been trying to avoid it and protect all of you from it."

"Funny, we all seemed to be involved." Damon extended his legs and crossed his arms, totally closing himself off to me.

"No, I was trying to avoid this exact situation, you know, where everyone places the blame on the wrong person. If the second set of tests had concurred with the first then I would have come to all of you. But if they came back proving false then no ones lives were destroyed."

"No one but mine, but hey, I don't count," Stella snapped.

"Well, you ended up destroying a lot more than you bargained for," Sophie added, her ire directed at me.

"I don't think I'm the one who created this mess, am I?" I turned to stare at Stella but instead was met by icy cold glares from not one but all of my brothers and their wives.

"You should have known better than to think those silly tests were accurate. Really, Tristan Nicholas, I'm disappointed in you." Mana clicked her tongue.

"Jesus, Mana, I'm a doctor and believe it or not it's

seldom that these tests are inaccurate. DNA doesn't lie, they can't be manipulated. The only possibility was human error. So I had to look at it from both sides. One side telling me that there was no way this could be true and the other saying, these tests don't lie and that I was sleeping with my half-sister."

"But your father? Tristan, how could you think such things of him?"

"Believe me, that was hard, I didn't want to. But I also didn't want to have that niggling doubt in my head. I'd seen the medical results, I now needed to see something medical to contradict it." I shoved my hands into my hair. This was going nowhere. One thing was coming from this family talk and that was . . . I was now public enemy number one. "But, Mana, when Stella and I came back, we overheard you saying on the phone that we were going to find out."

"What? That makes no sense."

"You were standing over there in the kitchen. You were whispering on the phone to someone, and you told them that we were going to find out."

"I said your names? I said Tristan and Stella are going to find out?"

I thought about that and then looked over to Stella, who was shaking her head. "No, she didn't say our names. We don't know that it had anything to do with this." Stella threw me under the bus. Hell, she was the one who created this entire mess by not keeping her fucking mouth shut, so why should I expect anything less.

I turned to face my mother, she'd lost it, seriously lost it this time and was laughing almost hysterically. "Why is this so funny?"

"That will teach you not to eavesdrop. I was talking to your aunt Dion. She was trying to order something for Leo and Ian before it sold out and wanted to know if they were going to have a boy or girl. I told her they didn't know yet but they were going to find out, as in the sex of the baby."

"Stella, I'm sorry that you're being pulled through all of this, but I'm not your father if that's what you're thinking. If it weren't for the fact that he looks like me and I saw him be born, I wouldn't think that he was ours the way he's been acting," Pops said, giving me a disappointed look.

"I've had it. I'm tired of everyone blaming me. I'm trying to get to the bottom of this. I didn't want to bring this up, I wanted to wait until the second results came back, but some people can't keep their mouths shut. No, they have to try to ruin everyone's lives not just mine." I shot daggers at Stella.

"What the hell, Tristan, you were the one who talked to me about it?" Carter said, making my glare shift to him.

"Yeah, and how many people did you turn around and tell?"

He had the good sense to look away, mumbling, "You still shouldn't talk to your wife like that."

"Wife?" I scoffed. "Are you kidding me? She left me, not the other way around. I wasn't the one who packed my stuff and left without so much as a note. I wasn't the one who refused to take her calls or return her texts. Just like her broken promise to let me handle this, she broke her promise to love me forever. *She* gave up on us, not me." My cheeks were burning from the heat of my anger. "That whole for better or worse meant nothing, she wasn't even willing to wait a few weeks while we sorted this out."

"Stop." Stella's voice didn't penetrate my anger. "Don't."

"He doesn't mean it." Katy's soothing words to Stella didn't cut through my mind, not at that moment. "He's just mad."

Shouts rang out, but I didn't turn to see who was hollering or what was going on. I just kept my head down as

I rested my hands on my knees and tried to regain some control of my temper. That was until I heard the door slam.

I shoved to my feet because this was total bullshit.

"Sit down," Pops demanded.

"I love you, *moro mou*, but this is your mess up," Mana said.

"How can you say that? You're all pissed that I didn't have faith in my family, but you totally sided with Stella and didn't even consider my side."

My family, the people I trusted to always have my back, were blaming me for Stella leaving. It made the bile in my stomach churn, and I knew that if I didn't get out of this room and away from them, I was going to say something I would never be able to take back.

There was a chorus of people yelling, telling me to come back so we could talk about this, but I was done. I couldn't sit there and let them all point the finger at me when I'd done nothing . . . nothing but try to protect them all.

I would go home, wait for the results, and then deal with my family later. As for Stella? Well, she'd already shown me exactly how much I meant to her and how willing she was to stand by my side, which was to say that she wasn't willing at all.

I punctuated that thought by slamming the front door behind me as I left.

STELLA

Sweat poured off me as I rummaged through my boxes in my storage unit. One of these suckers had to have my diploma, but which one I had no clue. *Where are you?* I grabbed another file box and regretted it. Propping my back against the metal waffled wall, I slid down and rested on my haunches. I flipped through photos from Ariel's wedding where Tristan and I danced together, Ian and Leo's wedding where we walked hand in hand, and more pictures from Sophie and Carter and Katy and Damon where Tristan and I had been paired together over and over again.

God! I hated all of this. I hate you, Tristan Christakos, I hate the day I ever met you and your gorgeous body all six feet two inches of well-built . . . man. Ugh.

Putting the photos away, I dug deeper and finally felt relief when I saw it. Perfect. I was officially ready to start my job at Wolfson Children's Hospital. After I snapped a photo of my diploma, I emailed it to my contact at HR at Wolfson and then headed home. I had the movers coming on Saturday to load my stuff and take it to my new apartment in Jacksonville. Since I'd only seen the place online, I was a little apprehensive about it, but I needed somewhere to stay and no time to see the place beforehand.

My townhouse was still empty since I hadn't really moved back in, which was kind of depressing, but I went there anyway, grabbing my mail on my way past the community mailboxes. All but three pieces of it were junk, so I sat on my empty counter and opened the first letter, which was from Wolfson. It was my official offer letter with my appointment to Children's oncology. I'd never worked in oncology, but I loved children a lot more than most adults, so it was going to be good.

I grabbed the next letter and groaned. It was from Tander Genetics. As if they hadn't ruined my life enough. Sliding one nail under the edge of the seal, I ripped it open and pulled out the letter. It looked like a basic form letter.

DEAR VALUED CUSTOMER,

We are writing to inform you of a recent discovery of a minor discrepancy that may have compromised some of our genetic reports. If you've received a letter with a case number ending in 05.27 your report may be one of those that was generated during the time of the glitch and, as such, received an inaccurate reading.

We are also sending you this letter to describe the services we are offering to help relieve concerns and restore your confidence in us.

Be assured that we keep no tissue or blood samples on file, and we have destroyed all records. We would like to offer you a complete autosomal genetic panel test again at no charge.

Your business is of the utmost importance to us, and we hope that you put your trust in Tander Genetics once again.

We assure you that we are committed to providing the best services in Medical Laboratory results.

We look forward to your future business.

Sincerely,

Joel Kirnapper

President/ CEO

I READ and then re-read the letter.

You have to be fucking kidding me.

I started laughing. I curled into a ball on my side and tears poured down my cheeks as the funniest unfunny thing ever had ruined my entire fucking life.

I got it, I totally got how people went postal, it was always over shit like this, wasn't it? Someone else fucks them over, messes up their life, and then thinks the world should go back to being hunky-fucking-dory. Why? What did I ever do to them? I wasn't sure who I was talking to, but I had so many emotions I needed to let them out.

My phone dinged, and I didn't answer it.

I got up and grabbed a pillow, swinging it against the back door. Beating the shit out of it. "How dare you do this to me?" Thwack. Smash. "Your lab took everything." Slam. "My friends." Thwack. "My family." Smash. "The love of my life and our promised future." Smack, smack, smack.

My phone dinged again and again.

I seriously considered tossing it against the door as well until I saw the name on the text: Tristan.

TRISTAN: I got the new results back. Call me.

Tristan: Just got home, did you get the letter from Tander? Call me.

Tristan: Call me, please. I love you.

197

. . .

"You love me? No, you don't!" I shouted at the top of my lungs. "You were more worried about everyone else than you were about us. Priorities, Mr. Christakos, you let me know that I'd never come first. I deserved to be someone's priority. If you'd only kept me, we could have figured this out together. But nooo, it became you against me and protecting them. Aghhh!" I picked up the pillow again and began smacking it against the door, the wall, my bed, the floor.

I didn't stop until after I was standing amidst a flurry of feathers. Then I started laughing. My living room looked like the Stay Puff Marshmallow guy had exploded, white puffy shit was everywhere, and my pillow? Well, it was just a shell of a pillow that was empty, no more stuffing.

THE NEXT MORNING, I met with the realtor and the couple buying my townhome at the closing office. By noon, I no longer owned any property—hell, I had very few bills since my car was paid off. This wouldn't last long, I was moving into my new apartment this weekend.

As I drove over to my brother's house, my gut clenched when I drove by Tristan's house and saw his Lexus in the driveway. I had no clue what he was doing home since this was his normal workday.

Stay out of it, it's none of my business what he's doing home, he isn't my concern. Stay focused and just go to Carter's.

TRISTAN

*T*only knew one thing, and that was that I had to get Stella back.

So, I sent her a text.

Me: Want to go to dinner?

MY HEART PICKED up speed when three little dots appeared.

STELLA: Can't, I'm spending time with my nieces.

I WAITED a few minutes then sent another message.

Me: Want to go back to Vegas?
    Stella: LOL, no.
    Me: Greece?

Stella: Stop.

I WAS LOST, I had no clue what to do, so I went to talk to the one person who I could always count on. I just hoped that she was still talking to me. As I walked up to the door, a weird feeling broke over me, should I knock? Oh my god, I was thirty-six and had never knocked on this door in my entire life, why now?

Because I screwed up and am wondering if I can make things right.

I hated it when my brain was more aware of the situation than my heart was. Pressing the lever on the handle, I pushed the door open to my childhood home and walked in.

"Mana, Pops, it's me, can I come in?"

Pops was standing in the kitchen, his arms were wrapped around Mana, and I felt like an intruder. "Come here, *moro mou.*" Mana waved me over as she opened the circle between her and Pops. "You silly boy. I love you, but at times, you infuriate me. All of you do." She squeezed me tighter, and Pops never let go. Suddenly, I was a kid again, walking in and catching my parents kissing and them bringing me in to squeeze me. They used to do it to all of us, and sometimes, to all of us at once.

"*Stafyli,*" I whispered, calling us grapes in Greek just like Mana used to when we were all bunched together like this. She would say that it was because we made something sweet.

"I messed everything up, didn't I?"

"Best thing about families, we always forgive you," Pops assured me.

"What about Stella? I don't think she's going to forgive me."

"Big mistakes deserve even bigger apologies. I'll leave you two to talk." Pops gave Mana another kiss and then they brought me in for one more hug. "Wait, before you go. I'm sorry." I pulled out both letters and handed them to my dad. "What are these?"

"Letters, one is from Tander Genetics with results from that second test. As expected, only Christakos are related and only Stella and Carter are related."

"And the other letter?" Pops didn't read them, he trusted me to tell him.

"An apology letter from the company that says there was a mistake with the first letter. Here, you can read them."

"I don't need to read them, I could have told you there was a mistake and that the four of you and only the four of you belong to your mother and me. We don't have any other children; although, we love your wives like our own, they are not our flesh and blood, just you four. Trust me, son, if you learn one thing from all of this, I hope that you learned trust and to trust those who you love."

Mana laughed. "Didn't I tell you?"

"I'll be out in the garage." Pops headed out.

"Sit, what's on your mind?" Mana moved into the kitchen and grabbed a plate. Dishing up a piece of baklava onto it, she grabbed a fork and brought it over before setting it in front of me. "So, how big are we talking?"

STELLA

"*H*ello?"

"Is this Stella Lang?"

God, that question cut me, I'd dreamed of being Christakos. "Yes, it is."

"This is Abel Jackson from Wolfson Children's Hospital, do you have a moment to talk?"

"Sure, what can I do for you, Mr. Jackson?"

"I work in human resources, and I'm calling because you were hired to work in our oncology unit, but we wanted to know if you'd be willing to switch to neonatal instead. Your resume shows that you have experience in neonatal."

"That's fine, I actually love neonatal, but when I interviewed, you didn't have an open position."

"At the time, we were looking for a new neonatologist and had planned to let that person build his own team, and we just found one. As a matter of fact, that was how we discovered your experience in neonatology."

"What? I don't understand."

"The new doctor has requested you to work with him, it was one of his hiring contingencies."

"I'm still not following. I don't know any doctors in Jacksonville."

"No, actually the doctor is from Orlando, from your existing hospital."

An ominous feeling washed over me. "May I ask who I'll be working with?"

"Absolutely, Dr. Tristan Christakos. He's a younger doctor, but he says that you two work wonderfully together. Well, we look forward to seeing you on Monday. Thank you, Miss Lang."

I disconnected the call and stormed out of Carter's front door and right to Tristan's.

He must have been expecting me because before I could ring the bell, he swung the door open.

"You weren't going to ring, were you? This is your house, after all."

"No, it isn't, it's yours. Would you care to tell me what the hell you're playing at?"

"What do you mean?" He smirked. I wanted to reach up and smack the shit-eating grin right off his smug fucking face.

"You know damn well what I mean. Wolfson, requesting me. You can't."

"I can, and I did."

"Your home is here."

"So is yours, but you're leaving it."

"Your family is here."

"No. My family is wherever you are. If you're in Jacksonville, then so am I." Tristan folded his arms and leaned against the wall. He was not blocking the doorway, no, he was making it perfectly clear that it was wide open for me to come in. Hell with that, I wasn't falling for that trap, no way, not again.

"I failed you once. I didn't put us first, and I'm going to correct that. I'll do whatever it takes."

"Nothing. There's nothing you can do."

"I don't believe you. You love me, I know that you still do."

"I do love you, Tristan, but this time, I have to love myself more. I can't put myself through it again. I can't get ripped to shreds. I can't wait for the next time I become the thing you're willing to sacrifice. Not when I'd sacrifice anything for you. Common sense told us this was a mistake—"

"Oh, I got the new results back and they concurred, it was a mistake."

"That only adds fuel to the fire. Our marriage was salvageable four weeks ago when all you had to do was ask your pops, it was simple. Those two keep no secrets. But . . ."

"But I wasn't thinking straight, I'd just received some crazy-ass letter and was losing the love of my life."

"Yeah, you were, you were thinking that you knew me less time than you'd known them so I was expendable. Guess what, I'll always be that person, which means that I'll never come first."

"I'm not giving up on us."

"You already did."

If truths were knives, then I'd just slaughtered myself and left myself open, exposed, and bleeding.

STELLA

"Thank you for coming with me." Sophie smiled as she held my hand and walked toward Christine and George's. She was wearing one of her typical sundresses, but I was in jeans. If this was a going away party for me, then, damn it, I got to decide what I was wearing, and comfort was key. That and most of my shit was already packed. "You're awfully quiet."

I stared down at Avril, who was toddling in front of me and pulling me by the hem of my shirt. The difference in our sizes made it hard for me not to trip over her.

"I'm mentally preparing myself."

"For what?" Sophie acted all innocent but she knew as well as me what.

"Saying goodbye to all of you and being in the same room as he-who-must-not-be-named."

"Voldemort?" Harlow, Sophie's eight-year-old daughter, asked.

I smiled. "Yeah, Voldemort, the Dark Lord." I laughed, and Harlow, Gianna, and Avril giggled.

When I got into the house, my stress over Tristan eased

and I was happy to see all of my friends there, all of the Iron Orchids, and Ringo.

"Hey, girl, why do you look so sad?"

"There won't be anyone around to keep them all in line, you'll have to keep the torch going for me." I stopped talking at the sound of music and everyone quickly scattered like cockroaches in bright light.

I followed them out the door that led to the backyard and not the pool and froze. Standing down by the lake, underneath a trellis was the most gorgeous man in a tuxedo, my man. Or, the man who used to be mine.

I took several hesitant steps as I tried to take in what exactly was going on. The music stopped, and I realized for the first time that Tristan was holding a microphone. All of our friends were standing holding drinks and they made a semi-circle that opened up so that all the focus was just on the two of us.

"Stella, over the last several weeks, you've shed a lot of tears, and that hurts me. It hurts me, not only do I know that I'm a big cause for it, but also because you're always the first one to laugh. You always have a smile for everyone. And lately that spark has been gone and well, the world has been a little darker because of it. I promise that I will do everything in my power to make you always smile and laugh even if it is at the most inopportune times. I know, that isn't my norm, but I want to show you that, for you, I'd do anything."

My legs were shaking, I wanted to run to him, but at the same time, I knew that I couldn't handle being broken again, not by him. He'd almost destroyed me, and I allowed it because I loved him so completely.

"In Vegas, we said vows, but they were canned vows, not original and definitely not ones that would make you smile. So, keeping true to my word, starting now, which is the most inopportune time, I want to show you my love and make you laugh all at the same time."

Tristan took one step toward me, speakers cracked, and music started to play. I smiled as he got down on one knee and lip-synced "I Want to Hold Your Hand" by the Beatles for a few lines, and when it got to the part about me letting him be the man, the music changed and Tristan crooned along with Bob Dylan's "To Make You Feel My Love." When the song got to the line about not making my mind up yet, I knew that it was a lie because I had. There could never be anyone for me but this man.

Tristan took another step closer as the music changed once more, I gasped because he knew that I loved this song. Shania Twain was my spirit animal; she was strong and mighty. He slowly walked toward me, not bothering to look at our friends and family gathered around watching this. Instead, he sang the song that fit like perfectly written wedding vows, "From This Moment On." When it got to the chorus, he was standing in front of me, and I wanted to jump in his arms but then he would stop singing, and I didn't want that.

But when Tristan took my hand in his and said, "And now for the big finish." The speakers popped, the music volume turned up, and Whitney Houston along with the man of my dreams belted "I Will Always Love You."

I wanted to say my vows, I wanted to do this with him right now but not in jeans and a T-shirt. Turning around I ran inside. I had to get home. I needed to change into my dress. Oh, shit, where was my dress? Was it in storage?

"Stella, where are you going?" Sophie hollered as she tried to keep up with me.

"I got to go."

"Where? What are you doing?"

My mind was going a million miles a minute. "The storage, I have to get to the storage place."

"Why?"

"My dress, I have to get my dress. Tristan's waiting for me." I looked up and everything was blurry as I tried to see her through my tear filled eyes. "Please, I have to get my dress before he leaves and thinks that I don't love him. Please, Sophie, help me."

"Stella, come with me. Your dress is in his old bedroom, I had Carter go find it for you." I threw my arms around her.

"Help me, please help me."

"Of course."

I turned to pull her down the hallway and caught sight of Tristan standing in the open French doors. "I'd wait forever. Take your time, I'll be the man in the tux."

He'd wait, oh my god. My husband, I was getting my husband back, my family. Oh my god. Running into Tristan's old room, I ripped my shirt off and was toeing off my shoes before Sophie had time to close the door.

Less than fifteen minutes later, I was pushing open the French doors and felt the firm grip of my brother stopping me. "Slow down, spider monkey. I didn't get to walk you down the first time, so I'm walking you this time."

Carter and I walked through the doors, and I saw him, my Greek god with that smirk on his face. "Carter, I love you and I love that you want to walk me down, but this is something that I need to do in my style."

"Go for it, spider monkey." I loved that he used his nickname for me even when I was dressed up all fancy. Carter let go of my arm, I kicked off my gorgeous shoes that Tristan had bought me in Vegas, and I ran to the man of my dreams, throwing myself into his arms, wrapping my legs around him, and lowering my mouth to his.

I wasn't sure who, but someone said, "You may now kiss the bride."

"Does this mean that you'll stay and not move to Jacksonville?"

"Fine, I'll stay, now will you shut up and kiss me?" I felt Tristan's lips lift into his signature smirk as he pressed his mouth to mine.

EPILOGUE

 ix months later . . .

"Better late than never. How are you feeling, Mrs. Christakos?"

I turned and looked over my shoulder.

"What are you looking for?"

"To see if your mother is here. When I hear Mrs. Christakos, I think of Christine. Plus, we're in Greece, there's probably a hundred of them."

Tristan laughed. "But there is only one Mrs. Christakos to me."

I leaned over and kissed him. "Feeling fine now. I was queasy on the flight, but I'm better now."

"Let's go inside for a while, too much sun isn't good for the baby." Tristan petted my belly . . . he fucking petted it like I was a lamb or a llama in a petting zoo. He must have noticed the scowl on my face because he whipped his hand back and let it drop to his side.

"Sorry, I just get so excited knowing that our son—"

"Daughter."

"Or daughter is in there. I was going to say that if you'd only let me finish."

"But why do you always say son first? Daughter comes first in alphabetical order. Why do guys always go first, hmmm, why?" I loved doing this to him, I was in the mood for ice cream, and when I went off on one of my "tangents" as he called them, he always offered ice cream, chocolate, whatever I wanted. "Is this why the queen always has to protect the precious king in chess? Hmm? Is this why you decided that we had to have a king-sized bed? Because guys were better than women? Is that what you're trying to say? I don't know, Tristan, what has come over you, but—"

"Would you like some ice cream? I think that there's some of the lemon custard that you like."

I pretended to be pouting and nodded.

"Okay, I'll be right back."

"And that, my darling daughter, is why women have all the power." I rubbed my belly then stretched out languidly on the chaise lounge. We'd been in Crete for a week, but this was our last day. Even though it was our honeymoon, Tristan wanted to take me to Mykonos to meet some of his family there.

I looked up toward the bright sun, but it was blocked by my very own Greek god standing over me offering me ice cream. "Have you decided when or how you want to tell my parents that we're expecting?"

"I figured we don't say anything and see who has the biggest balls to comment that I'm gaining weight. You know they'll be torn between curiosity and self-preservation."

"This, right here"—Tristan pointed at me—"this is why I keep hoping for a son. The thought of a daughter scares the shit out of me. She'd be you only worse because she wouldn't have to learn from scratch. No, she'd be in advanced Jedi classes from day one."

I pinched my lips to fight my smile.

"Yeah, go ahead and laugh. I'm imagining the fights that I'm going to get into when someone tells me to control my kid, then you're going to jump in, and then I'm going to defend both of my girls."

His girls. God, I love how that sounded. "Mr. Christakos, I think you're right, I've had enough sun for the day. Let's do something else."

"What do you have in mind?" He wiggled his eyebrows.

I could already see where his mind was going, but we weren't technically newlyweds, we were just on a vacation. True, it was our first since getting married, we wanted to come before this, but there just never seemed to be enough time. Once we got the hospital to hire me back and officially move me into the role as Tristan's medical assistant so we could work on the genetic center, and we saw this as our chance. "Let's go into the town center, I want to get a few souvenirs, and maybe I'll find some adorable baby stuff."

TWO MONTHS LATER . . .

"OKAY, Mom and Dad, you ready to see the baby?" Dr. Granger asked. She was the only obstetrician that Tristan would even consider. She was the best according to him. "We're ready." I squeezed Tristan's hand.

She squirted some warm jelly onto my stomach and rolled the transducer across my skin. Her busy little fingers went to work, clicking away on the keyboard, and I watched as Tristan smiled. Then a sound filled the room.

"Whoa, hold on, doc, that isn't right." I turned to Tristan, who was laughing, fucking laughing. "Don't you dare start laughing, Tristan, I will geld you right here." I turned my attention to the doctor. "Fix it. I know what I'm hearing—fix it, fix it right now. This isn't funny. I don't know what kind of prank you're playing, but this isn't funny."

"Stella, this isn't a prank, that's definitely two heartbeats you're hearing."

"Why didn't you tell me this the first time? What kind of crackpot doctor are you? I want a second opinion, I know all too well why you call your medical offices practices, you all are still practicing. I've been given wrong information once before, not again. Nope, no way."

"Calm down, Stella. It's common to miss the second heartbeat early on. Many times they are still so faint or so rapid that the two are in sync." Tristan wrapped his arms around me and whispered into my ear, "Calm down, love, we got this. We can handle anything, we've already proved that."

"Would you two like to know what you're having?" Dr. Granger asked.

"Yes," Tristan replied.

"Why not." I gave a flip of my wrist.

"Lie back, Stella." Dr. Granger rolled the transducer some more and pressed down even more. "One of your babies tends to be a little shy, the little one isn't letting us get a full frontal image." She placed a hand on my stomach and lightly massaged.

"Shy? Well then we know that can't be a daughter," Tristan said under his breath, I gave him my stink-eye.

"Well, this, right here, is your daughter." Dr. Granger pointed to one of the two babies. "Look at her, she wants you to see her."

"So do we name her little Stella now since of the two she is obviously the showman?"

"Bite me," I snapped.

"Come on, baby number two, your mommy and daddy want to see you." Dr. Granger's words warmed me all over. Mommy, I was going to be a mommy. Damn straight, and I'd be the best mommy ever, nothing like my mom. "There he is."

"He?" Tristan asked.

"Yep, you're having fraternal twins, a girl and a boy." Dr. Granger continued clicking and taking photos of the ultrasound images while I gazed at the two little peanuts on the screen.

"Okay, I have all the images that I need. I will leave these up, Tristan, if you want to hold the transducer for a few minutes, I'll give you two a few minutes alone."

"Thanks, Olivia." Tristan held the tool steady and we waited until she left the room. "So, are you happy?"

"Yes and scared."

"Don't be, I've got you. I've got all three of you."

"Forever?"

"For always."

———————————

Can Vivian's drunk-dialed wrong number be her Mr. Right? Find out in ***Vivian, Midnight Call Girl***.

Continue flipping the pages in this book for a sneak peek of Vivian, Midnight Call Girl and to find a list of all of my books.

SNEAK PEEK—VIVIAN, MIDNIGHT CALL GIRL

BOOK 6, IRON ORCHIDS

Prologue - Vivian

"*D*on't get up, baby." Eric leaned over to kiss me. "Today you have got to make a decision about where you want to go. Honey, we are less than six months away from our five-year wedding anniversary, and I don't want to spend it here."

"I know, I know. I promise," I said as I leaned up to meet him halfway. Eric and I had been high school sweethearts, even though he was two years older. Even when he went off to college, he came home every weekend to see me. Our love was a forever type of love; sometimes I had to pinch myself to prove that this was my life and not some dream. "Can I make you something to eat before you go into work?"

"Sleep, I've got it." Eric kissed me again. "I love you." The smell of Irish Spring soap lingered even after he pulled away.

"Love you too. Be safe."

Eric paused in the open doorway of our bedroom. "Always."

I closed my eyes and nestled back into my warm covers to

get a few more hours of shut-eye. Sliding one hand over to his pillow, I squeezed it and then tucked it under my chin. The cold cotton was soothing as I fell back to sleep.

I sat straight up to the sound of my doorbell and then glanced at the clock on my nightstand. Shit, it was after nine.

I jumped out of bed just as my doorbell rang again. "I'm coming." I raced through the house as I finger-combed my hair. I pulled open the door and paused at the sight of two of Eric's best friends and fellow deputies. They were standing there, not smiling. "Hey, Kayson, Carter . . ." They didn't say anything, it all happened in slow motion. Kayson reached forward, my sleep-addled mind cleared, my knees buckled, and my world crashed down around me.

FIND ME

Website: www.daniellenorman.com

Official Iron Orchids Reading Group : www.daniellenor-man.com/group

Sign up for Danielle's Newsletter and stay in the know
Newsletter: www.daniellenorman.com/news

Find Me on TikTok

Guess What—I have my very own Ap.
There, you can peruse my book selections or find me at book signings. You will also get early notifications of sales or releases or any other trick I might have up my sleeve. Just tap the link below to download from your preferred Ap Store.
Apple Store
Google Play

SUGGESTED READING ORDER

IRON ORCHIDS, BOOKS 1 THROUGH 7 AND THE BOX SETS, ALL IN KINDLE UNLIMITED.
Take a group of wild crazy females and mix them with some very sexy hot guys and you have yourself a great series in the making.

Ariel, Always Enough - Book 1
Sophie, Almost Mine - Book 2
Katy, My Impact - Book 3
Leo, Kiss Often - Book 4
Stella, Until You - Book 5
Vivian, Midnight Call Girl - Book 6
Ringo, Slippery Banana - Book 7

IRON ORCHIDS BOX SET COLLECTION

Iron Orchids, Box Set 1 - Ariel, Always Enough and *Sophie, Almost Mine*
Iron Orchids, Box Set 2 - Katy, My Impact and *Leo, Kiss Often*

Iron Orchids, Box Set 3 - Stella, Until You and *Vivian, Midnight Call Girl*

Iron Badges, Books 1 through 5

You met some of them in the Iron Orchids. Now these women motorcycle officers will ride into your heart.

Sadie, Doctor Accident - Book 1
Bridget, Federal Protection - Book 2
Piper, Unlikely Outlaw - Book 3
Kat, Knight Watch - Book 4
Harley, Stealing Happiness Book 5

Blood Roses

A group of women who are bound by their belief for doing what's right. They're the Black-Hat side of the Badges but they take care of business just the same. Discover what happened to each of these women that united them as a gang of vigilantes.

Kobe, Bad Blood - Book 1 (Coming April 13, 2021)
India, Cold Blood (TBA)
Astrid, Blood Money (TBA)

Iron Ladies, Books 1 through 4
"Here, take this, you need it."
It was the sacred code of a whisper network of women.
The wives of controlling husbands.
The partners of cheating men.
Women who'd been helped by The Iron Ladies.

Adeline, Getting Even - Book 1
Sunday, Sweet Vengeance - Book 2

Melanie, Delivering Karma - Book 3
Olivia, Striking Back - Book 4 (Coming June 15, 2021)

IRON HORSE, BOOKS 1 THROUGH 3

Three sisters take charge of the family ranch after their father dies, eager to show the world that the strongest cowboys are women.

London, Is Falling - Book 1
Paris, In Love - Book 2
Holland, At War - Book 3

STAND ALONES

Roads Traveled an ever growing collection of short stories and novellas from Danielle Norman.

A WORD FROM DANIELLE

*T*hank you for picking up my book. It doesn't matter whether you have read one book of twenty written by me, they all have some commonalities to them:

Strong women with attitude.

Alpha heroes who love them anyway.

And a strong bond of friendship that we all need in our lives.

The Iron Orchids, books 1 through 7, were my original series of romance novels. Each book can be read as a standalone. What connects the stories are the fact the same people appear and eventually each gets their own Happily Ever After.

So if you've read one then you are probably dying to read about the rest of the brothers and their missing cousin.

Read on to find sneak peeks from some of the books along with my suggested reading order.

Thank you again - Dani

MEET DANIELLE

*D*anielle began her career as a children's author where her books earned acclaim on several lists for bestselling author. Not to mention Library Guild awards and STEM award author of the year.

BUT HER BELIEFS have always been that vodka, high heels, and a well-spoken F-word could solve almost any problem. Unfortunately those things aren't the foundation for kids books. So, she switched her name (Danielle is her middle name, Norman is her husband) to protect the innocent and started writing romance, nothing like strong women, hot men, and steamy action.

THANK YOU

- Editing by Ashley Williams- AW Editing
- Proofread by Julie Deaton- Deaton Author Services
- Alpha Reader- Peggy Monroe

To my Iron Orchids gang and Alexis and Abbie for keeping it active, thank you. Y'all make the place the first place I want to go each morning when I click on my computer.

I never imagined finding a group of people just as warped in the head as me. God, I love y'all, you make me laugh every day.

CHEERS,
Dani

Made in the USA
Middletown, DE
07 September 2023

38118204R00135